BARRY GIFFORD was born in Chicago in 1946. He is the author of over twenty-five books – ranging over the genres of fiction, non-fiction, poetry, plays and screenplays – and his work has been translated into over seventeen languages. His novel, *Wild at Heart* (made into an award-winning film by David Lynch) was the first in a succession of novels exploring the contemporary American landscape that have brought him increasing international acclaim.

Gifford's writing has also appeared in many magazines and newspapers and his books have received numerous literary awards. One of them, *Night People*, was presented the Premio Brancati, Italy's national book award, established by Pier Paolo Pasolini and Alberto Moravia.

He lives in the San Francisco Bay area.

By the same author

FICTION
The Sinaloa Story
Baby Cat-Face
Arise and Walk
Night People

The Sailor and Lula Novels:
Wild at Heart
Perdita Durango
Sailor's Holiday
Sultans of Africa
Consuelo's Kiss
Bad Day for the Leopard Man

New Mysteries of Paris
Port Tropique
Landscape with Traveler
A Boy's Novel

NONFICTION
Bordertown (with David Perry)
The Phantom Father: A Memoir
A Day at the Races
The Devil Thumbs a Ride &
Other Unforgettable Films
The Neighborhood of Baseball
Saroyan: A Biography
(with Lawrence Lee)
Jack's Book: An Oral Biography of
Jack Kerouac (with Lawrence Lee)

POETRY
Flaubert at Key West
Ghosts No Horse Can Carry
Giotto's Circle
Beautiful Phantoms
Persimmons: Poems for Paintings
The Boy You Have Always Loved
Poems from Snail Hut
Horse hauling timber out of
Hokkaido forest
Coyote Tantras
The Blood of the Parade
Selected Poems of Francis Jammes
(translations, with Bettina Dickie)

PLAYS
Hotel Room Trilogy

SCREENPLAYS
Lost Highway (with David Lynch)

MUSIC
Madrugada: A Libretto for
Toru Takemitsu

BARRY GIFFORD

THE SINALOA STORY

REBEL inc.

First published in Great Britain in 1998 by Rebel Inc.,
an imprint of
Canongate Books Ltd,
14 High Street,
Edinburgh EH1 1TE

First published in the USA in 1998 by
Harcourt Brace & Company

10 9 8 7 6 5 4 3 2 1

Book Design by Linda Lockowitz

British Library Cataloguing-in-Publication Data
A catalogue record for this book is available
on request from the British Library

ISBN 0 86241 805 4

Rebel Inc. series editor: Kevin Williamson

Printed and bound by
Caledonian International,
Bishopbriggs, Glasgow

For Michael Swindle

I am waiting for death.
—SAINT AUGUSTINE

I lay down last night
on the wrong side of town.
—DON COVAY

PRELUDE

THE MOTHER
OF THE LIGHT

THE INTERIOR of a house. A dim hallway, lit only by extremely low-watt bulbs. The hallway is silent, empty. A door opens and a small man emerges from a room. He is carrying a hat. He closes the door to the room, puts on his hat and walks to the far end of the hallway, turns left and disappears. The sound of a woman's voice faintly enters the passageway: A record is playing somewhere in the house, Yolanda del Rio singing *"Tus Maletas en la Puerta."* Suddenly there is a loud noise, a *thump*, followed by an agonized cry. More thumps follow, then a louder cry. Two short, thick-shouldered men appear at the distant end of the hallway. They hurry down the corridor toward the source of the noise. They enter a room off the corridor—*not* the room the man with the hat departed—and there is a shout, a muffled yell, several thudding sounds, body punches. The two thick-shouldered men appear again in the hallway, holding between them another man, whose legs are not working. The thick-shouldered men hold the seemingly lifeless man under his armpits as they drag him away along the corridor. They turn left at the end of the hall and disappear from view. The door to the room from which the limp man was taken remains open, spilling an additional sliver of pale light into the corridor. Quiet sobs are coming from the room, inside of which a small brown girl, no older than sixteen, sits naked on a narrow cot, crying. Her thick black hair falls far below her shoulders. Bruises are visible on her face and upper arms. There is a mirrored dresser next to the bed. Religious items festoon the mirror: rosary beads, silver chains with dangling crucifixes, postcard pictures of various saints stuck into the sides between glass and frame. On the other side of the room is a washbasin, next to that a toilet. Yolanda del Rio is singing *"Hoy Te Toca Dormir en el Suelo."* The girl stands, her shoulders shaking, chest heaving, eyes streaming. She rises unsteadily, walks with small, tentative steps toward the door, and slowly closes it.

PART ONE

SINALOA

DELRAY AND AVA

A WRINKLED RIBBON of blue lightning lit up the landscape like a birthday cake. DelRay Mudo was driving on the outskirts of Sinaloa, Texas, listening to Dr. Nuca Picabia's tape *The Losing Battle Against Low Self-Esteem and How Not to Fight It*. "I do not like people of taste," snarled the former Santo Domingo horse doctor who'd turned psychologist to the masses via cable television; "they remind me of game hung too long."

In Nuca Picabia, DelRay thought, the Mexican bandit and revolutionary Pancho Villa would have found a genuine companion. Both were rugged individualists, leaders, men from humble backgrounds who despised elitism and despotism, however those evils might be disguised. When Villa assumed control of the government of Chihuahua in 1913, he ordered that any Spaniard caught within the boundaries of that state would be escorted to the nearest wall by a firing squad. When the American consul objected to what seemed to him an irrational and savage policy decision, Villa responded: "Señor Consul, we Mexicans have had three hundred years of the Spaniards. They have not changed in character since the conquistadores. They disrupted the Indian Empire and enslaved the people. We did not ask them to mingle their blood with ours. Twice we drove them out of Mexico and allowed them to return with the same rights as Mexicans, and they used these rights to steal away our land, to make the people slaves, and to take up arms against the cause of liberty... They thrust on us the greatest superstition the world has ever known—the Catholic Church. They ought to be killed for that alone."

The horse doctor advocated assassination as an antidote to proselytizers of organized religion, a prescription with which DelRay Mudo could not disagree. The problem with religion, thought DelRay, was that it had no soul. Señor Picabia's panegyric, however, wore him out after twenty minutes or so, and DelRay turned off the tape and tuned in his favorite local radio station, KILO.

"How do, South Texas," a crackly male voice announced. "Rumors are flyin' that Excello's Red Devil service station will not be here in Sinaloa much longer. Well, sir, this is Excello Pomus himself speakin', and I own the property at number eight Gorch Street, as recorded in the chancery clerk's office, Comanche County courthouse. The next time I move, Sparky and Buddy's Funeral Home and Dump Truck Rental will be in charge. Any real questions, call me—Excello Pomus, owner and operator of Excello's Red Devil, 555-1814, in Sinaloa, Texas. Thank you, and praise the Lord."

"Thank you, Excello," came a youthful male voice. "Hope that straightens out *that* situation. Got one more announcement, this from Pellejo y Hijo Pet Food. We pay for dead livestock, restaurant grease, and store meat scraps. Toll-free long distance. In Texas, the number is 1-800-555-HOOF. That's 1-800-555-4663. Outside the great state, it's 1-800-55-MOUTH. That's right, 1-800-556-6884."

Heavy water hit the windshield, followed by a whipcrack of lightning that blinded DelRay and caused

him to lose control of the car momentarily. DelRay
switched off the ignition and glided to a complete stop
on the shoulder of the road. Mudo needed some
downtime to consider his situation anyway, seeing as
how it was at least as serious as the weather.

He thought about Ava Varazo and wondered
where she was. The last time DelRay had seen her,
Ava was wearing the green scarf with purple and
yellow parrots on it that he had bought for her in
Nogales. If she were here now, with him in the
Cutlass, he might have a hard time deciding whether
to strangle her or fuck her. He would probably do
both, but he could not be certain of the order of
events.

Ava Varazo was working as a carhop whore at
Puma Charlie's Eat-It and Beat-It, a drive-in on the
outskirts of La Paz, Arizona, when she met DelRay
Mudo. He had heard about the Puma, as it was fa-
miliarly known, for several months before checking
out what his long-haul trucker buddies said was the
finest cathouse upside the border. Puma Charlie, who
passed himself off as part Quechua Indian on his Bolivian mother's side, was actually a Sicilian-American
named Carmine Ricobene, born and raised in the
Belmont neighborhood of Queens, New York City.

Puma Charlie had fled the East Coast, where the mob put a price on his head for pulling a double cross during a drug deal, and landed in the southwestern bordertown of La Paz, pimping.

The drive-in was a sweet setup—the state police and INS agents took *la mordida* half in flesh, half in cash, with the occasional cheeseburger or piece of pie thrown in as lagniappe. Customers parked their vehicles in stalls and ordered blondes, brunettes or redheads over an intercom, specifying preference for shape, height, etc. If they were regulars, the men had only to mention the name of their choice morsel, and they would be informed as to her availability. If a customer were required to wait longer than twenty minutes, a burger with onion rings or fries and a soft drink was provided free of charge. The Eat-It and Beat-It employed mostly illegal aliens, young girls smuggled in from Mexico, whom Puma Charlie housed in trailers behind the drive-in.

The former Queens racketeer had named his establishment and himself after the Andean myth that eclipses of the sun are caused by its being devoured by a puma. "My Bolivian grandmother, *mi abuela*, told me," the erstwhile Carmine Ricobene liked to lie to customers, "that an eclipse means the sun is sick. Our people, the Quechua, would light fires to warm the earth, and children would scream and shout and beat animals with sticks to make them cry out, in order to frighten the puma away."

Ava Varazo had come from the tiny town of La Villanía, forty miles south of the border. Legend had it that the pueblo's name ("the despicable act") derived from a slaughter of defenseless women and children by U.S. soldiers on that spot during the Mexican-American War in 1847. Ever since then, Ava had told DelRay, women from her village had within their hearts a murderous agenda where gringos were concerned.

"You mean I'd better watch out," DelRay joked.

"I mean you'd better watch out for me," said Ava.

DelRay Mudo had chosen Ava Varazo from among the other carhops because of the way the early-evening redness highlighted her practically waist-length silky black hair. Her nickname at the Puma was La Crin, "the horse's mane." None of the prostitutes had naturally colored hair other than black, she told DelRay, and since he patronized only Ava, he had no basis by which to disbelieve her.

DelRay was living in Phoenix when he met Ava, working as a mechanic at Chifla Miguel's Motorcycle

Repair on Fifty-eighth Street in Guadalupe. It was Ava who convinced him to quit his dead-end gig at Chifla Miguel's and do something meaningful with his life.

"Like what?" DelRay asked her, as they lay on freshly soiled sheets in Ava's Airstream, listening to the Carrier drone.

"Help me run a number on a rich pimp I know in Texas. Then we get married, have kids, make a life together."

"My daddy, Domingo 'Duro' Mudo, used to say, 'The Lord's rule is nothin' good ever happens in Texas.' "

Ava licked the sweat beads on DelRay's chest, then stuck the tip of her tongue into his right ear.

"No disrespect to your father, *mi amor*," she whispered, "but maybe God will make an exception in this case."

EAST TO SINALOA

SO THEY WENT TO Sinaloa, Texas, unemployed DelRay
and his marvelous, evil Ava. What *was* so marvelous
about her, mused DelRay as he nudged the Cutlass
forward. Not only her coal-lustrous mane, reptilian
green eyes, thumb-length knife scar high on her left
cheek that glowed amber when she got hot—it was
the way Ava *moved* that captured DelRay. Her head,
her hips, her *mobility*. All of Ava. DelRay lit up an
unfiltered Lucky Strike and replayed the Sinaloa story
in his head, hoping to make sense of it.

"Indio Desacato is a dangerous man," Ava had
warned DelRay before they left La Paz. "But he's
hooked on me. Hooked on a hooker. Funny, huh?"

"Like me," said DelRay.

"Right, honey. Only with a difference."

"What's that?"

"I'm with you, not him."

Ava kissed DelRay and he kissed back. They were sitting in the front seat of his car, parked next to the gas pumps at Plata Argentina's Mercury Service Station. Mudo had just fueled up preparatory to their leaving La Paz.

"I guess I'm a lucky boy, then."

"What, you think you're not?"

DelRay fired the Cutlass and headed out.

"Tell me again about this deal."

"Dope, baby. Indio Desacato got a chain of whore-houses across Texas. He lives in Sinaloa, near the bor-der, on a fancy estate."

"You been there?"

"No, but he told me about it. Indio invited me to come live with him."

"Why didn't you go before?"

"Because he's a beast. Beats his girls. Famous for it. Always treated me good when he come to La Paz, but I know that wouldn't last once he got me to Texas."

"What about Puma Charlie?"

"Charlie's easy about it. Girls want to go, he lets 'em. More comin' in all the time from Mexico. Ain't exactly a shortage of women wantin' to work."

"So how you figure we can take this Desacato? Given that he's such a dangerous character."

"S-H-C."

"S-what?"

"S-H-C. Spontaneous human combustion. After we take out his safe, we're gonna nail him and make it look like he exploded. Read about an hombre stopped his car by a road, got out to bleed his snake, and all of a sudden glowed blue before collapsing dead on the ground."

"Who saw this happen?"

"His wife, who was in the car. She didn't want to touch his body because it was smokin'. Cops called the medical people, who discovered a hole in the guy's stomach, which had turned to carbon."

"What?!"

"Yeah. Apparently an electrical current of some kind had entered his body through the earth and caused him to spontaneously combust, right where he stood with his snake in his hand. Scientists later said he mighta been electrocuted from his piss, which coulda acted as a conductor of the electricity. Turns out he was takin' a leak underneath power lines in open country. There's invisible electrical fields all around places like that, and the charge jumped right up inside his prick, calcified his internal organs. None of this could be a hundred percent verified, of course, so they called it SHC. I figure we can make Desacato's death look like a case of spontaneous human combustion."

"You're a more complicated woman than I thought," said DelRay.

Ava laughed and tossed her mane. "What you think can make you crazy," she said.

ELIJAH'S ANGEL

INDIO'S MAIN MAN in Sinaloa, a one-eyed, six-foot-seven, 380-pound former professional football player named Thankful Priest, took care of the day-to-day business operations, leaving Desacato free to travel and recruit. Thankful Priest once asked his boss how it was that the whorehouse flourished regardless of shifts in local government. Indio Desacato just laughed and said, "Elijah outran the chariot of King Ahab, boy. Remember that."

Thankful Priest's Christian name had been chosen by his mother, Jezebel Bone Toussaint, so that he would be forever reminded of man's need to be beholden to the Lord for his place on earth. Thankful's father, Arturo Okazaki Priest, a half Mexican, half Hawaiian-Japanese pilot, had died two months prior to his son's birth when the crop duster he was flying was struck by a twelve-stroke lightning flash over Big Tuna, Texas, igniting the tank's mixture of oxygen and fuel vapor.

Thankful's athletic career had been cut short after he enucleated his own left eyeball from its socket two hours after ingesting Ecstasy at a team party. Thankful popped the eyeball from his head and used a Bugeye Bob Fish Skinner to sever the connective muscles and tendons before collapsing on the kitchen floor in the house of his teammate, all-pro offensive tackle Frank "Fighting Chicken" Chicarelli. After doctors failed to reattach his orb, Priest told police investigating the incident that the eyeball had imprinted upon it a pentagram, a five-pointed star he believed to be the sign of Satan.

Indio Desacato's primary method of bringing girls into the country was simply to marry them in Mexico and drive them across the border. On his next trip to Mexico he would obtain, with the woman's written and witnessed consent, a divorce. He married only the "special" girls, however, women Indio knew would attract a high-paying clientele. Other women heard about his operation and presented themselves for an audition.

Indio had been extraordinarily taken with Ava Varazo the first time he saw her in that La Paz pesthole. When Puma Charlie called him and said she was coming, Desacato told Charlie he would compensate him generously. Puma Charlie said it wasn't necessary but that he appreciated the thought. "My thought will be in your hands the day after she shows up," said Indio.

Indio thought about a black Labrador retriever named Andy who used to walk with him to school every day when he was a kid in Waxahachie. Andy belonged to a neighbor but he loved Indio, who always fed his lunch to the dog on the way to school. Indio would take another student's lunch for himself. Ava Varazo reminded Indio of Andy. She was lively and beautiful, sleek and dark like that Lab, and he assumed that as long as he fed her well, as the Lord's angel did Elijah, she would remain just as loyal.

ONLY THE LONELY
KNOW TIME

HAND PRINTED ON a board nailed to the wall behind the front desk of the Tom Horn Hotel on Ethiopia Street in Sinaloa were the words, "Love ye therefore the stranger: for ye were strangers in the land of Egypt. —Deut. 10:19."

DelRay had taken a room on the third floor. He now sat in the lobby, smoking a Lucky, waiting to hear from Ava, whom he had dropped off at Indio Desacato's mansion. The Tom Horn was an old hotel, built in 1910. Never a particularly grand idea, the lobby was nevertheless spacious, and large ceiling fans spun wearily but noiselessly above the several old men seated in the scattered maroon leather armchairs that occupied the room.

"First time in Sinaloa?"

DelRay turned his head twenty-two degrees to the west and identified his would-be interlocutor, an octogenarian gentleman outfitted in a shiny double-breasted blue suit with a longhorn string tie. The old man's hands and face were littered with liver spots the size of Susan B. Anthonys.

"Yes, sir," answered DelRay. "First time."

"I was born here in Sinaloa, same year as this hotel opened for business. Both the Tom Horn and I are eighty-five come October. What's this, September?"

"September nineteen."

"October last, that's me. Day Jeff Davis died."

The man extended his calico right hand.

"Name is Smith, Arkadelphia Quantrill Smith. Call me Arky."

"DelRay Mudo. Call me Del."

The two men shook hands. DelRay was impressed by the strength in the old fellow's fingers.

"Quite a grip you got there, Arky. Quite a name, too."

Arky chortled. "My grandpap rode with Shelby in the Iron Brigade. You heard of them, I suppose."

"No, sir, can't say as I have."

"Durin' the Unpleasantness this was—War Between the States—about this month of 'sixty-three—that's *eighteen* sixty-three—Cap'n Jo Shelby and his six hundred, includin' my grandpappy, Dockery 'Doc' Smith, started out at Arkadelphia—my nameplace—crossed the Arkansas River into Missouri, where they was joined by as many or more border Confederates, and proceeded to whup Yankee butt, burn bridges and supply posts, and disrupt lines of communication clear to Boonville. Shelby's cavalry disguised themselves by wearin' Union uniforms with sprigs of red sumac in their hats, which was supposed to be the secret sign identifyin' Federal troops. Oh, Shelby's boys foxed 'em good! In forty-one days the Iron Brigade destroyed millions of dollars of Union rollin' stock and comestibles, killed and wounded hundreds of Yankee soldiers, and made it back to Arkansas with more men than they'd started with. Those Missouri bushwhackers signed on with Shelby in a New York minute."

"Quite a story, Mr. Smith."

"The endin', of course, ain't so glorified."

"How's that?"

"They was drove down into Texas, finally. At Cascadia, Shelby knew the cause was lost but he refused to surrender. Two hundred men followed him into Mexico, where Maximilian, the Austrian puppet put into power by the French, who'd driven out Benito Juárez, was kindly disposed toward the Confederacy. On the way Shelby's troopers stopped to wrap their bullet-riddled flags around rocks and buried 'em in the Rio Grande."

"What happened to them in Mexico?"

"Maximilian offered 'em some land around Vera Cruz, and a few went there. Others just used Mexico as a restin' place before movin' on to Cuba and Brazil, where they was welcome. Maximilian got drove out of Old Mexico not long later, though. The French got scared by the Union Army, led by Little Phil Sheridan, that gathered at the border, and abandoned Maximilian. Soon as Juárez retook Mexico City, the Johnny Rebs who'd settled at Vera Cruz took off, includin' Doc Smith. He come up to Brownsville, where he was recruited by Rip Ford for McCook's command that regulated Messican bandits around Old Sal del Rey. Wasn't 'til later he moved up to Sinaloa. That was after he married my grandmother, Quintana Fayette Quantrill, who was an illegitimate daughter of Colonel William Quantrill—though she used his name—the man who led the bloody raid on Lawrence, Kansas, where a hundred and fifty people were murdered in their beds."

DelRay lit a new Lucky off the old one.

"Those were some days, I guess," he said.

"Ferocious times, son," said Arkadelphia Smith. "Now, my own parents, Stand and Quantrilla McCurly Smith, they run a feed store until they died, and I run it after them. Sold it to a man named Ramos ten years ago. Daddy was named after Stand Watie, a mixed-blood Cherokee who become a Confederate brigadier general and was the last officer to surrender his command. My mother was mixed-blood herself, part Messican on her daddy's side and French Negro on her mama's—man named Francis Xavier Bonaparte, fought with the Second Kansas Colored Infantry, all I know."

"You know a hell of a lot about back in the days, Mr. Smith."

"Call me Arky. Only the lonely know time, son. Sixty years from now—provided the planet got sixty big ones left in her—you won't disagree, I bet."

The late-afternoon sun had diminished considerably while DelRay listened. Only the slenderest rays slithered through the heavy blinds fixed over the front windows of the hotel lobby. DelRay was startled by a

sudden loud snore. He glanced west and saw that
Arkadelphia Quantrill Smith was sound asleep in his
chair. DelRay wondered what Ava Varazo was up to
with Indio Desacato right now.

"I'm sure I won't, Arky," he said.

THE BIG EMPTY

"ONLY TWO WAYS to run a business—the *right* way and the *wrong* way. Trick is, of course, knowing which's which before it's too late. There are people on the street would rather shoot you than say good-evening."

Indio Desacato sat alone on an immaculate white couch, smoking a Royal Jamaica.

"My experience," responded Ava Varazo, who stood by a picture window staring out at acres of arid land, holding a tequila sunrise in her right hand, "men don't get to choose the direction their dicks bend."

She sipped her sunrise through a plastic accordion straw and shook her mane.

"Uh-uh," she said. "Just look at all that nothin'

out there. You know how New Orleans is called the Big Easy? Well, southwest Texas ought to be called the Big Empty."

Indio laughed. "Lots of bones buried out there, makin' crude."

"What I mean," said Ava.

"I'm pleased to have you with me, Ava. This is not a decision you'll regret. You will be the highest-priced girl in my domain."

"And here I been dreamin' maybe you had the idea to make an honest woman of me."

Desacato laughed harder than before. "Nobody is honest, Ava. Each person knows this if he is honest with himself."

"All that 'he' and 'him.' You wouldn't think there was really such a being as a woman to begin with."

"Sure, a woman started everything—and a man will finish it."

"Of that I never had no doubt," said Ava.

Indio was a wide-shouldered man, stocky, short but powerful, a few weeks shy of his fortieth birthday. His face was the shade of Madeira and his orbital cavities so sunken that sometimes it seemed as if he hadn't any eyes. Before he spoke he licked the ends of his trim mustache.

"Come to me, *chica*. Show me what I'm paying for."

Ava glared at him for a moment, then softened. "You got it comin', okay," she said, then finished her drink with one swallow.

Indio unzipped his trousers and took out his cock. It was short and thick, mud-colored like the rest of him. Ava thought Desacato's dick resembled a turd.

"Come, pretty," he said.

Ava put down her glass on a table, walked over, knelt in front of him and pretended that she was eating shit. Indio closed his eyes and pictured the buttocks of a nine-year-old girl wearing tight red shorts who he had seen the day before bending over to drink from a water fountain.

SAINTS PRESERVE US

AVA HAD A thumbnail-sized scar high on her left cheek. When DelRay inquired about it she turned sullen and the pink mark became crimson. A shudder, visible to Mudo, passed through the length of her body, concluding with a brief facial twist and audible soft gasp. At the moment, the two were semi-entwined, standing under a xanthic desert moon in front of Ava's trailer.

"You know what day this is?" asked Ava.

"February twenty-ninth," he said. "Had a extra day before rent's due."

"El Día de Santa Niña de las Putas, the patron saint of Satan's prisoners. It comes only when there is a second full moon in the month on the final day of February in a leap year."

"Knew about the blue moon. Never heard of Satan's prisoners, though."

"Those are souls sold to Satan during the person's lifetime. People who reformed before their death and tried to undo the deal."

DelRay disentwined himself, lit a Lucky, inhaled, coughed. The night air felt chilly now that he wasn't pressed against Ava. He rubbed his hands together, then shoved them into his pants pockets, letting the cigarette dangle from between his lips.

"Who was Santa Niña?" he mumbled.

"A peasant girl, like me," said Ava, "born in Huehuetenango, Guatemala. Her father had bargained with the devil in order to save the life of his wife, who was dying from a cancer. Satan told him his wife would live only if the man promised also the souls of his three sons."

"Not the daughter?"

"Niña was not yet born. She was the youngest of four children. The father was horrified to do this but consented, thinking that later he could persuade Satan not to take his sons. The mother recovered and, of course, no matter how passionately her husband begged, the devil would not relent. The thought that he and his sons were doomed to hell destroyed the poor man, and he died of grief soon after the birth of his daughter."

"Did the mother know about this deal?"

"Not until her husband confessed on his deathbed. When Niña was twelve years old her brothers were killed when a donkey cart in which they were riding broke its axle on a steep mountain road and crashed with the donkey to the bottom of a ravine. Niña's mother then told her about the fate of the boys' souls, so the girl vowed to save them and her father."

DelRay spat out the cigarette. "Did she?"

"Yes. That night she called to Satan, telling him she could not live without her brothers, that she wanted to join them immediately. When Satan appeared she took his hand and allowed him to lead her to hell, where she became his mistress."

"No shit!" Suddenly DelRay no longer felt the cold.

"Satan's attachment to Niña was soon complete. She beguiled him in ways even the King of Cruelty had never imagined. In this way was it possible for her to gain a kind of power over the devil and convince him to allow her father and brothers to pass out of hell and enter into the Kingdom of Heaven. Niña, of course, had to remain in hell as Satan's whore. It is the prostitutes who honor her on this, the rarest of days, for her sacrifice."

"Saint Niña of the Whores."

"Our own and only. This is the one day no whore should feel ashamed in the eyes of God."

"But what about your scar? How did you get it?"

"After I was fucked by a man for money for the first time I cut myself on the face with the sharp edge of a rock."

"But why? You were so beautiful.—You still are, of course."

"To never be as beautiful again. I was marked inside and out."

DelRay embraced her. "My poor Ava."

She pulled away and glared at him. "No," she said, "there is nothing about me that is poor."

Drugstore Cowboys

THANKFUL PRIEST strode boldly into Zambo Fike's Farmacia Cafe and deposited his considerable bulk on two well-worn red leatherette stools. Zambo, whose real name was Jesus Maria, had earned his nickname from his part-time job as a rodeo clown whose specialty was to hop spread-legged directly over the horns of a Brahma bull. He had discontinued this secondary occupation several years before, after a particularly unruly dun-colored beast named Ygdrasill had speared the pharmacologist-clown's left testicle as Zambo was attempting a fingertip three-sixty. Zambo kept a photograph of Ygdrasill tacked to the wall behind the toilet in his establishment, so that every time he took a piss he could remind himself why he had quit rodeoing.

"Gimme some beans and beer and pray nobody's near!" Thankful shouted at the toad-faced, bowlegged proprietor who stood behind the counter sucking on a bad crook. "Hell, Zambo, time you treated yourself to a decent-smellin' smoke, don't you think?"

"These suit me, Thankful," said Zambo, staring as he always did at Priest's discolored glass eye. Thankful had once accidentally dropped the eye into an open can of magenta paint. He had cleaned it but the eye was permanently tinted and gave his face a peculiar, otherworldly glow, adding to his already menacing appearance.

DelRay Mudo had been standing by the magazine rack, leafing through the latest issue of *Trackdown*, the monthly report about activities of bounty hunters, when Thankful Priest entered. After ordering his lunch, the monster noticed DelRay reading the magazine.

"Sinaloa ain't got no regular library," Thankful said. "Zambo's be it."

DelRay looked up and stared at him. "Pardon me?"

"I said, you fixin' to buy that magazine?"

"What business is it of yours if I do or don't?"

"Hey, Zambo, this skinny crust of white trash is in my face over an innocent remark. I want you should remember that when the sheriff asks how come there's a bloody pile of dogshit used to once maybe been some measly type of person on your floor here."

"You got to fool with it, Thankful, take it outside. Don't need no drugstore cowboys bustin' the place up."

"How about it, pardner?" Thankful Priest said to DelRay Mudo.

"How about what?" asked DelRay.

"We take it to the street."

DelRay replaced *Trackdown* in the rack, looked at the cockeyed hulk spread over the better part of two stools, and said, "You must be the famous Polyphemus I've heard about."

"Polly who?" Thankful laughed. "Do I look like a Polly to you?"

DelRay went to the door and opened it.

"What's your name?" asked Priest.

"Ulysses," said DelRay, just before stepping out. "Keep an eye out for me."

A MESSAGE TO MUDO

DELRAY HAD NOT heard from Ava for almost a full week before Framboyán Lanzar delivered a message late one morning. Mudo was still in bed at the Tom Horn when there came two rapid taps on his door. DelRay was not asleep but he was in a bit of a trance, day-dreaming about Cherry Layne, a character in *Nurse's Night Off*, a paperback novel he'd been reading the night before. In the novel, Cherry Layne, a nubile young nurse in a big city hospital, has oral and/or anal sex with three different doctors, two interns, an anesthesiologist, and another female nurse during her first week on the job. All of these activities take place at the hospital, during her regular shift; DelRay had not yet gotten to her night off. Cherry refuses to have conventional sexual intercourse, saving herself, as she explains to her various partners, for marriage. "Only my husband, whoever he may turn out to be, can come through the front door," Cherry says to Dr. Ramses "Ram" Melville, an internationally renowned brain surgeon who monitors his own heartbeat through a stethoscope as he and Nurse Layne cavort standing at the bedside of a very recently deceased patient. DelRay was imagining himself tongueing Cherry's rosebud as a second set of rapid-fire taps pierced his reverie.

"Who's there?"

"*¡Un mensajero!*" said a voice from the hallway. "I have a message for Señor Mudo."

"*Uno momento.*"

DelRay reluctantly climbed out of bed, bending his half-master back into his undershorts, and went to the door. He was wearing a badly frayed and soiled T-shirt proclaiming Chifla Miguel Makes Motorcycles Mo' Better. DelRay opened the door and saw a short kid with a crewcut staring at him. The kid looked to be about sixteen or seventeen years old.

"A message for me?"

The kid bounced up and down on the balls of his feet as he said, "If your name's DelRay Mudo."

"I'm him."

"How I can be sure?" the vertically inclined kid asked. "Lady said be *certero*."

DelRay got his pants, pulled them on, and took his wallet out of a pocket. He showed the boy his driver's license.

"That proof enough?"

"Guess so."

DelRay replaced the wallet and said, "Where's the message?"

The kid kept hopping. "Not where, what."

"Why're you jumpin' up and down?"

"I'm a boxer. Framboyán Lanzar. Numero dos-ranked flyweight in West Texas. Exercisin' my feet muscles. Got a fight next month in San Angelo with Danny Melaza."

"Danny Molasses. I seen him fight Chuy Chancho in Nogales. Chancho was disqualified for tryin' to head-butt."

"Yeah, Chuy's a dirty fighter. But I gonna slow Melaza down to the ground!"

"So what's the message?"

"Lady said meet her at two o'clock this afternoon at El Oráculo."

"What's that? And what lady?"

"Lady with real long hair is supposed to be the highes'-price *puta* workin' now at La Casa Desacato. She tell me when I deliver the *cervezas* and whiskey. Pay me ten bucks."

"Where's El Oráculo?"

"South on old Highway 4, eight miles jus' about. Is a cantina next to the road. You can' miss it."

"Sounded like you got a pretty good jab, way you rap on the door."

Framboyán Lanzar shadowboxed and shuffled for a few seconds in the hotel corridor.

"Hey, man," he said, "how 'bout a tip?"

"Danny Molasses is always lookin' to lead with his right, so he's a sucker for a hook off the jab. *Buena suerte,*" said DelRay, and closed the door.

THE ORACLE

DELRAY FOUND El Oráculo without any trouble and was sitting at the bar with a Tecate in front of him by 1:45. He was anxious to see Ava Varazo. His body ached for hers, and he was eager to get on with their plan. DelRay's cash was running low; he wouldn't be able to afford his room at the Tom Horn for more than another week. For some reason he'd lost his taste for cigarettes and had not bought any for the last two days. That was one way to save a few bucks. Shit, once he and Ava took possession of Indio Desacato's 500K, they could buy a damn tobacco plantation.

DelRay had the can to his lips when "Viva Las Vegas" started to play on the jukebox. Elvis Presley was never a favorite of Mudo's, and he grimaced as the beer coursed through his system. DelRay set the can down on the counter and swiveled around on his stool to see who it was had spent good money on such a bad record. He immediately recognized the back of the huge man he had encountered in the Farmacia Cafe, the ornery, one-eyed giant the drugstore owner had called Thankful. The giant spilled a few more coins into the Rock-Ola before he turned and spotted DelRay.

Thankful's false eye reflected the variety of colors from the dozens of bottles displayed behind the bar. It was always his artificial orb that people looked at first and stared at while speaking to him, as if Thankful's functional one were unworthy of attention.

"Jesus," said Thankful, "if it ain't my old pal You...You..."

"Ulysses," said DelRay. "You've got a good memory."

"I remember bein' called Polly."

"Polyphemus. An old friend of mine you kind of resemble."

"Viva Las Vegas" blared from behind Thankful Priest.

"You like Elvis?" Priest asked.

DelRay shrugged. "Take him or leave him."

"This song's from a movie he done with Ann-Margret. I do believe El had him some of that! Mmmmm-mmm."

Thankful swayed to the music as if he were riding a surfboard. He closed his eyes and listened until the tune was finished, and he didn't reopen them until the next one started. DelRay was relieved to hear Bobby Bare singing "Six Days on the Road and I'm Gonna Make It Home Tonight," but he was a bit unsettled when Priest gathered together the two empty stools directly to DelRay's left and burdened them with his enormous bulk.

"Hey, Chino!" Thankful yelled to the bartender. "Bring me a triple shot of Gusano Rojo and two Tecates for a chaser." Then he focused his attention on DelRay and said, "Okay, You, fill me in on this cat Polyphemus."

DelRay looked at the clock on the wall above the mirror behind the bar and saw that it was five minutes until two.

"In Greek mythology, he was a big, tough guy. His family name was Cyclops."

"He was powerful, huh?"

"Very."

Thankful's drinks arrived and he dispatched the mezcal with one swallow, then chased it with half a beer. He belched loudly, just as Patsy Cline launched into "Walkin' After Midnight." DelRay's estimation of Thankful Priest's musical taste was steadily rising.

Ava Varazo saw DelRay engaged in conversation with Thankful and ducked quickly back outside. Indio forbade his girls to frequent El Oráculo or any other bar or honky-tonk in the area. His belief was that the women would remain more mysterious, more exotic, and therefore more desirable to the locals if kept out of public view. Control had more than a little to do with this edict, of course, an aspect of Indio's decree that made Ava very uncomfortable.

She had been treated well during the past month and felt that Indio had begun to trust her. Ava's idea was to insinuate herself into the gangster pimp's inner circle so as to more efficiently accomplish her goal. She knew it would be necessary to have an outside hand on the deal, which was why she had enlisted DelRay. Ava's long-range agenda did not necessarily include him.

Standing in the sun, leaning against the cantina wall, Ava thought about her village, La Villanía, the family and friends she had left behind. She hoped it

would not be too long before she saw them again.
Now she decided to wait until Thankful Priest left.
Ava retreated to the brown '78 Monte Carlo with
extra-dark tinted windows she had borrowed from
Moke Lamer, the handyman at La Casa Desacato.
Moke had a hard crush on her, and Ava was certainly
not above exploiting it. All he had asked of Ava was
that she allow him to lick the instep of her left foot,
which she had. This kind of creepy request did nothing
to elevate Ava's opinion of men.

Inside the cantina, Priest and Mudo had begun
to feel comfortable in one another's company. They
bought each other several beers and traded off feeding
the juke. DelRay's anxiety over hooking up with Ava
vanished in the alcohol-induced haze. After more than
an hour of steady drinking, Thankful slid off the two
stools and announced that he had to depart.

"You're all right, amigo," Thankful said to DelRay,
clapping him on the back with a grizzly-sized paw.
"I'm sure we'll meet again soon."

"Count on it," said DelRay.

Thankful Priest stumbled out into the sunlight.
DelRay gathered himself and headed for the men's
room. He was in midstream when he heard Ava's
voice.

"Drinking with the enemy, huh?"

DelRay began to turn, then realized he was still in the act of micturition, which he did not disrupt.

"Shit, baby, I thought you was never gonna come."

"I heard that before."

Mudo finished pissing, buttoned up, and faced La Crin. She looked more beautiful to him than ever, and he went to embrace her. Ava backed away.

"Don't you know who you been hangin' out with?" she asked.

"Yeah. Old Polyphemus himself. The Cyclops."

"Look, fool, that's Thankful Priest, Indio's top gun. I hope you didn't tell him nothin' about why you're here."

"No. Hell, I told him I was an unemployed mechanic, driftin' through. That ain't far off the truth." DelRay moved toward her again. "Hey, honey, how you been? I missed you bad."

Ava allowed him to hug and rub against her.

"Let's get out of this stinking place," she said.

Ava led DelRay out to the Monte Carlo and told him to get in on the passenger side. She slid behind the wheel.

"Whose short is this?"

"Belongs to a guy does odd jobs around La Casa. He's okay, he won't say nothin'."

"Made some good friends already, I guess."

"Baby, here's what you gotta do."

"Gotta do somethin' pretty soon, since I'm about out of coin."

"I know. I'll have Framboyán bring you some money, but you have to be patient. I'm gettin' close to Indio. It's just a matter of time before I can catch the combination to his safe. I found out where it is, in the floor under his bed."

"You been doin' the time with him, huh?"

DelRay was sobering up fast.

Ava did not blink. "Only what's necessary, Del. You and me are in this together. *Por vida.*"

"*Por vida.*"

Ava slid over and kissed DelRay tenderly on his *cerveza*-swollen lips.

"Let's go to the hotel, Ava."

"I can't, honey. I'm away too long now. I'll come to see you there as soon as I can, I promise. I'm workin' out a plan how to take Indio down. You got to trust me, Del."

DelRay looked at her lovely dark face as clearly as he could. There were tiny yellow crosses in her sienna eyes.

"I trust you, Ava."

She kissed him again and put her hand between his legs, cupping his balls with her fingers. "I need what you got, too, baby," she said.

DelRay got out of the car and stood in front of El Oráculo and watched Ava drive away. For a moment, weaving slightly in the gravel dust of the Monte Carlo's kick, the drunken feeling returned and he didn't know what to do. DelRay was dizzy and sat down on a wooden parking stub. He stared at the ground in front of him and saw the face of Jesus Christ. DelRay closed his eyes hard, then reopened them and looked again. The face was still there, only now it was covered with blood, the redness running over the white stones onto his boots. DelRay leaped up and ran into the bar.

TRINITY

"MY MAMA NAMED ME after Chino Cortina, the Almighty's nominee to chase the Norteamericanos out of Texas and restore it to the Mexican union."

"When was this?"

"When my mama named me?"

"No, when this other Chino was around."

"Oh, from the 1840s, '50s. After the Mexican-American War."

DelRay was the last of the afternoon customers in El Oráculo. He was nursing his eleventh beer, building up the nerve to tell Chino, the bartender, about having seen Christ's bleeding face on the gravel in the parking lot.

"This Cortina led a gang of *liberadores* that terrorized Americanos from Laredo to the Gulf of Mexico.
He was the bad kid from a good family. Couldn't read
or write. The poor people loved him."

"Kind of like Robin Hood, huh?"

"That's right. I was born on the same day,
September 28, that Cortina's desperadoes raided Río
Grande City. They looted the American businesses,
shouting, 'Death to all *gringos!*' "

DelRay polished off his beer. Chino popped open
another Tecate, set it down in front of him and said,
"No charge, brother."

"So what happened next?"

"His marauders was expected to attack Brazos
Santiago and Point Isabel, the shipping depots for
Brownsville, so the Texas Rangers raided his encamp-
ment. Had them a vicious battle before daylight.
Heavy fog made it difficult to tell Americans from
Mexicans. Everybody was shootin' at everybody. Fi-
nally the Rangers drove Cortina's men into the river.
The fog lifted and the Texans cut down Chino's boys
with Sharpe's rifles like buffaloes as they were wading
across."

" 'Bout Cortina?"

"Ah, El Chino escaped. Got to Guerrero, in

Mexico, with thirty of his five hundred men. He kept up his campaign, built a new army of *guerrilleros*, and vowed to fight for the emancipation of *peóns* along the border. Cortina mounted another big raid into Texas in 1861, but mostly his outfit just hit and run. He died in 1894. On his deathbed Chino swore that even in heaven or hell, wherever he encountered *los gringos apestosos*, his name would be written in blood and fire."

DelRay's eyes were closed as he tipped the can of Tecate to his lips, but he was too drunk to swallow and the beer drooled down the front of his shirt.

"Blood," he said. "Jesus. Stinking *gringos*."

DelRay's head thudded down on the bar. Chino crossed himself and let it lie.

MOO YANG

AVA WAS GIVING HEAD to a seventy-one-year-old beet farmer from Big Spring named Euple Mapes when she heard the gunshot. Euple's prostate problems being what they were, he was about at the point that a fair piss beat hell out of having what could reasonably be considered a decent erection. Ava had been working on Euple's penis a good fifteen minutes without any discernible sign of blood gathering in the tissue when he lit up a cigarette and said, "Give it another few licks, missy, and if the old warhorse don't stir I'll settle for a high five in the rectum." The explosion came right after that.

Both Ava and the john jumped at the sound. Euple Mapes stood and pulled up his pants. Ava went to the door, opened it a crack, and peered into the corridor. Thankful Priest pounded past and barged into a room two doors down and across the hall. Ava threw on a terry-cloth robe and followed him.

Thankful was standing just inside the room, and Ava poked her head in next to his right shoulder. Moo Yang, a fourteen-year-old Thai-Chinese girl Indio had brought in the week before from Port Arthur, was sitting on the floor holding a .44 Ruger Blackhawk with both hands, wearing only a buffalo horn head-dress. A man clothed in white buckskin and knee-high moccasins lay face down on the bed; the back of his head had mostly adhered to the wall directly above him. Ava, who had taken a liking to Moo Yang, squeezed past Priest and knelt next to the girl, who sat staring vacantly into space.

"¡Madre de Dios, niña!" said Ava. "What happened?"

Moo Yang lifted the revolver slowly and pointed it unsteadily at Thankful, who turned and fled.

"Pow!" she said, then lowered the big gun to her lap, resting the long black barrel along her smooth brown thigh.

"Moo Yang, *dime!*"

The girl smiled and looked at Ava Varazo. Her huge black eyes were glassy. She began to weep but kept smiling.

"America sucks," said Moo Yang.

A SHORT VISIT TO LA VIUDA

INDIO DESACATO controlled the steering wheel with the index and second fingers of his left hand. He guided his rainforest green Lincoln Mark VIII slowly through the dusty postmidnight streets of Ciudad Yeguada, six kilometers northwest of Tampico. Indio had heard about a house operated by a woman called La Viuda, "the Widow," who offered no whore more than twelve years old. He thought that a very young girl would be a special attraction in Sinaloa, especially if it were known that her residency was temporary. Indio had sent word to La Viuda and received a reply that she would be willing to rent out one of her *brotes* for a short time. She was expecting him.

At the end of what some dreamer or fool of a city planner had named Avenida de la Paz Eterna, as if such a backwater required or deserved an avenue, the predatory flesh merchant turned right, as he had been instructed, and brought the Mark VIII to a stop in front of a squat tin-roofed bungalow. Before getting out of the car, he opened the glove compartment and removed from it a nine-millimeter Glock automatic pistol. He put the pistol into the right side pocket of his safari jacket and surveyed the empty street. It was the time between Sunday night and Monday morning, *madrugada*, the hour between dog and wolf; and all of the dogs and wolves, the men who worked on the oil rigs, the men who worked in the bank or the courthouse, the cops, the ones who could afford to patronize La Casa de la Viuda, were obliged to honor the only night of the week that the establishment remained closed. Indio knew this and did not expect trouble, but he nevertheless felt more secure carrying a weapon. One never knew when an ugly dragon would appear bearing the unwelcome gift of fire breathing, especially in Mexico.

"Welcome, Mr. Desacato," said a handsome woman of approximately sixty years old, as Indio approached the bungalow entrance. The woman was dressed simply; she wore a long white cotton dress and had wrapped a black silk mantilla decorated with orange birds and scarlet flowers around her shoulders. "It's a pleasure to have you here."

"You must be La Viuda."

"I am, yes. Come in."

La Viuda closed the door behind him.

"You've come a long way," she said.

"The thought of what might be awaiting me kept me entertained."

The interior light was dim, but Indio could see that the Widow's face gave evidence of a grave history. The many lines in her cheeks and forehead looked like they had been cut with the thin edge of a finely honed knife. Indio had no doubt that not a single drop of the blood and tears she had shed had been or ever would be forgotten by La Viuda or by those who had caused the wounds, if any were still alive.

"I regret that I have only a short time," said Indio, "to avail myself of your hospitality."

There appeared out of the dimness by the Widow's side a sylph in a short black dress. The sylph's red hair was twisted together on the top of her head, knotted to stand up as if by force of electric shock. Her skin was red, too, but darker. She was about four feet tall and weighed no more than seventy pounds.

"We call her Perla Roja," said La Viuda. " 'Red Pearl.' For obvious reasons. She'll be twelve years old in three weeks."

Indio moved closer to the girl and studied her. He had never seen a child so exquisite, so unblemished. Her eyes were huge yellow-black spheres from which shone an eerie light, a flame from a time unremembered before this terrible and dangerous moment. The entire room glowed amber, burnished by Perla's presence.

"Sssssssssss," hissed Indio, as he circled the child. "Truly, Widow, this is something beyond dreaming."

He touched Perla Roja's round, perfect face with the fingertips of his right hand, then dropped to his knees and caressed her bare feet, toes, ankles, calves, thighs, sliding a hand over her tight, trembling buttocks before standing again.

"Name your price," Indio said.

The girl grabbed the Glock from Desacato's jacket pocket, pointed it at the Widow, and pressed the trigger. Four rounds invaded La Viuda's body before the tiny *puta* turned the pistol toward herself and fired. Indio staggered and fell as a bullet tore through Red

Pearl's left eye socket, exited her posterior medulla oblongata, and creased Desacato's collarbone before burying itself between the almost-clasped hands of a genuflecting Juan Diego as represented on a wall calendar advertising Discoteca Orquidea Negra. Bathed in the blood of fallen females, the visitor shut his eyes and stared into the grinning face of a jaguar.

THE SADNESS EXPRESS

DELRAY SAT NEXT TO the window in the northeast corner of his room at the Tom Horn Hotel looking out at the sand hills to the southwest. The day was fading fast. He lit a Lucky and listened to the long, lugubrious, wobbly whistle of the southbound Piedras Negras Hi-Ball. DelRay had already grown used to this scorching cry from the evening freight. La Expresa Tristeza, the locals called it, or El Tormento. Every day at 6:56 P.M., they said, *la horca del diablo*—the devil's pitchfork—was driven a bit deeper into the soul. Mudo had begun to believe it, expecting but never quite being prepared for the whistle. He was always taken by surprise.

Waiting for Ava was not easy for him. As a child DelRay had often accompanied his daddy, Duro, on his rounds of the Phoenix area bars. While Duro drank and caroused, DelRay was made to sit outside on the curb or in the pickup, sometimes for hours at a time, staring at and being stared at by passersby. Sometimes kids picked fights with him, older kids, and DelRay often had to run away and sneak back later, hoping that his father had not left him behind. Duro's *juerga* inevitably ended in a brawl. DelRay's abiding mental picture of Duro—who died of a stab wound to the chest when DelRay was sixteen—was his daddy's bloodied face as the elder Mudo stumbled out of some dive. DelRay always told people who asked that his daddy had died from a heart attack. He never told them that Duro's heart had been attacked with a blade wielded by a drunken coyote in a bar named Rowdy Dave's Dream of Paradise on Encanto Street in Padre Luna, Arizona.

DelRay's mother, Lucía, had died from pneumonia when the boy was four. He barely remembered her. Duro, who stood four foot eleven and one-quarter inch without his boots, was a legendary figure on the midget rodeo circuit from Agua Prieta to San José. His best event, before alcoholism forced him to quit, had been bull riding. Duro made his bones beating the clock at Gila Bend on a terrible beast named Nasty At Night one day past his seventeenth birthday. When he wasn't rodeoing, Duro worked construction and did odd jobs. DelRay had been on his own since his daddy's death. Until his infatuation with Ava Varazo, he'd kept clear of attachments. Now he was waiting again.

Just as the thin xanthic line was squeezed away in the west, two rapid pops sounded in the corridor outside of DelRay's room. He heard a loud thump, footsteps, then nothing. DelRay stayed where he was. The room was dark. The telephone rang. DelRay reached over to the bedside table and picked up the receiver.

"Yes?"

"Honey, it's me. Ava."

"Darlin', where are you?"

"At the house. Listen, I only got a minute. Indio's been away, he's comin' back tonight. Word is there's a big meet happenin' here in a couple of days with gangsters from all over the place. Turns out Desacato's is the main cash drop for the Southwest. That's why the money's here. It ain't Indio's, it's the mob's. We've got to take it before these other guys do."

"How?"

"Tomorrow night you and I are gonna get it directly from Indio. I want you to show up at the house just after midnight. Pretend you're a customer."

"That won't be tough."

"Say you want the most expensive girl in the place. That'll be me."

"Of course."

"I'll let you know what happens after that, when we're alone."

"I can't hardly wait."

"Gotta go, baby. *Te adoro.*"

"I love you, too, Ava."

She hung up first. DelRay replaced the receiver, then walked over to the door without turning on a light. He listened for several moments before opening it. A body lay perfectly still on the floor a few yards away near the top of the staircase. DelRay looked around. The hallway was empty. He approached the body carefully, keeping an eye out for any kind of movement. DelRay bent over the inert form and saw that it was Framboyán Lanzar. Two small red holes had been drilled into his forehead, undoubtedly by projectiles fired from a small-caliber handgun, either a .25 or a .22. Thin rivulets of blood ran from the holes onto the tiles. Framboyán the flyweight was down for the count.

DelRay went back to his room and closed the door. Suddenly he felt a little stab in his ribs, and he winced. Sinaloa, DelRay decided, was definitely not the place in which he would choose to raise his family, if he ever had one.

WILD COUNTRY

ELVIN "EL" PAÍS had promised to help her and he would. He was fifty-four years old, five foot six and a half with his boots on, and 239 pounds naked, but he had most of his hair, now a mixture of dirty brown and gray, and the use of his stumpy but sturdy limbs. His arms were heavily muscled from construction work and heavy-equipment operation. El País realized he had very little to show financially for more than thirty-five years of hard labor. He and his wife of a quarter century, Ginger, had only one thousand dollars in their joint account at Sinaloa Savings, of which Elvin had felt justified in withdrawing half. He should probably have taken more, he thought, but it was best Ginger not remember him as being greedy.

When Moo Yang first asked him about the possibility of their running away together, El País was confused. How could he, a fifty-plus fat man, make a life with a tiny fourteen-year-old Thai-Chinese prostitute? El was also thrilled by the idea. His childless marriage to Ginger had long since lost any reason to continue. About the only activity Elvin and Ginger shared an interest in anymore was eating, and his meager earnings precluded any real adventures of a culinary nature. Neither of them had much imagination in that department, either. Chicken-fried steak, mashed potatoes with brown gravy, lemon cream pie and Dr Pepper had been their staple diet for decades. Ginger, Elvin guessed, passed the three-hundred-pound mark twenty years ago and never glanced back.

The most recent sexual encounter between them that he could recall occurred on Elvin's fiftieth birthday. Ginger bought him an issue of *Juggs* magazine and while he perused pictures of huge-breasted women she masturbated him with a dish towel soaked in a mixture of grape jelly and motor oil. Her friend Earlene Weld had told her about an article in *Cosmopolitan* concerning spicing up married folks' sex life that suggested using honey and oil as a marital aid; so, using what she had on hand, Ginger gave it a shot.

This episode, however, had an unfortunate conclusion. After Elvin came, he fell asleep and Ginger went to the bathroom to wash her hands. While she was gone red ants got into the jelly jar, which Ginger had left open on the floor next to the slumbering birthday boy, and from there the fiery, aggressive devils made a swift assault on his slathered genitals. It took Elvin several weeks to recover from the bites, the first two in Sinaloa Baptist Hospital, during which time urination was possible only through catheterization. This gruesome experience did little to inspire further sexual experimentation or research on the couple's part.

Thereafter Elvin availed himself of biweekly visits to La Casa Desacato for a blowjob. Until the arrival of Moo Yang, however, País was not inspired to move past this seemingly dead-end existence. Following the shooting incident involving Big Chief Buffalo Horn— for which action Moo Yang was found by police to be entirely justified—the Thai-Chinese teenager began plotting her escape. El País, she decided, was her nicest customer, as well as being the least complicated or sexually troublesome. When she asked him to run off with her, he agreed immediately. Moo Yang tried to give him a second blowjob that night but Elvin wasn't up to it. Every two weeks was his speed, he told her; that was enough for him. Moo Yang smiled then for the first time since she had left Port Arthur. El País was her man.

Moo Yang jumped out of a second-story rear window onto a mattress in the bed of Elvin's three-quarter-ton Ford pickup at five o'clock one morning. País sped away with the girl and all seemed right with the world until he realized that in his haste and excitement he had forgotten to fill the truck with gas. El stopped at Excello Pomus's Red Devil on the way out of town and was in the process of fueling the Ford when Thankful Priest cruised his vintage '69 Barracuda convertible into the station.

Priest pulled the 'Cuda alongside the Ford and said to País, "You got somethin' belongs to Señor Desacato."

Elvin dropped the gasoline hose and backed away. Indio's gigantic monocular henchman debarked, a hideous, dark, glinting object in hand.

"I was only tryna hep her out," País said.

"No hurt my hero!" shouted Moo Yang.

"Try this, hero," Thankful replied, and made *pad tai* of Moo Yang's guy with a street sweeper.

The girl leaped out of the truck and ran down the road. Thankful Priest caught up with her thirty seconds later, cutting in front with the 'Cuda.

"Come on, Moo Yang. Get in."

Moo Yang sank to her skinny knees on the cracked asphalt, holding her hands over her face. The sun was coming up. She started screaming.

LONELY TEARDROPS

THE EXECUTION by lethal injection of a double cop-killer
named Roy R-Boy Willis was scheduled for 5:42 A.M.,
the predicted crack of dawn. Willis, whose parents had
indeed named him Roy R-Boy on his birth certificate,
was a native of Sinaloa, Texas, a former high school
football star whose Sinaloa Sidewinders teams had finished number one in the state each of the three years
he had been their starting quarterback. As such, Roy
R-Boy, who subsequently played two injury-plagued
and therefore undistinguished seasons at Texas Christian University, was accorded legendary status among
football aficionados in the Lone Star state. In other

words, R-Boy, which is what virtually everyone in Texas called him, whether or not they were acquainted with Willis personally, was about as famous in that part of the country as a person is likely to get. Even Hard-Shell Baptists, in their heart of hearts, though they surely would have had to struggle mightily with themselves to do so, most probably had to admit that during his heyday R-Boy Willis was as dear to them as Jesus Our Savior.

That Willis had come to this disingenuous pass was a tragic circumstance no Sinaloan could easily reconcile. According to the article DelRay read in the two-day-old *San Antonio Light* he found abandoned on Arkadelphia Quantrill Smith's usual sitting chair in the Tom Horn lobby, while recovering from football injuries at TCU Roy R-Boy had secretly joined a white supremacy group called Christ's Teardrops, a brotherhood devoted to avenging what they determined to be "crimes of impurity."

Roy's parents were God-fearing Baptists, not evangelicals or charismatics, and had inculcated in their four children, of whom R-Boy was the oldest, only the standard prejudices of the day. They were at a loss to explain Roy's radical activities.

"R-Boy didn't never display a mean stripe," said Estheruth Willis, his mother. "His manners is right."

"I don't say shootin' down peace officers is correct," said Worth "Cakewalk" Willis, Roy's father, himself a former star running back at Southern Methodist, "but R-Boy believed in his mission and they got in the way. I guess R-Boy believed he had license from a higher order and acted accordingly."

After dropping out of college before his junior year, R-Boy had gone to work for a car rental company in Odessa owned by Bundren "War" Bond, a rabid supporter of Texas Christian football and, as was recently revealed, the financial foundation of Christ's Teardrops. As instruments of this Christian Right vigilante outfit, Roy R-Boy and his cohorts set fires to houses occupied by minorities—i.e., non-whites (including Jews)—in an effort "to drive them the hell out of Texas," as Bond said.

One night after torching a home in San Angelo in which six Yemeni-Americans, three of whom were children, perished in their beds, R-Boy and Spartacus "Sparky" Bond, War Bond's nephew, were spotted fleeing the scene by one of the victims' neighbors. The neighbor called the police and described R-Boy's black

Chevrolet Grand National with the license plate TEARS
R-US. The cops caught up to the murderers near
Ozona, where a high-speed gun battle ensued, result-
ing in the deaths of two state troopers and Sparky
Bond. R-Boy eluded capture until just outside Sinaloa,
where a roadblock had been set up in the belief that
Willis would head to his hometown to obtain getaway
money from his parents or hide out with old friends.

When he saw the roadblock R-Boy braked his
dust-cloaked Grand National to a stop, sat in it while
he watched troopers surround him with weapons
drawn, then gunned the engine. Fearing that Willis
would attempt to crash the blockade, officers opened
fire on his vehicle. The Grand National absorbed
ninety-six rounds during this barrage but its occupant
miraculously survived, sustaining only flesh wounds in
both upper arms and a bullet crease across the top of
his shaved head, on the crown of which had been
tattooed two blue tears.

Roy R-Boy refused to communicate with anyone,
including his parents, from the moment of his capture
until five years later, three days prior to his execution,
when he wrote out for public release this statement:
"You have swung wide the Gates of Hell and allowed

Satan's Terrorists to dwell among His own. You have sentenced yourselves to an early death as surely as you have condemned me who would be your servant. Eternal shame be upon those cowards who stand in silent witness as the last Teardrops fall."

AVA'S DREAM

AVA HAD A DREAM in which she was riding on a bus in Mexico City—a place she imagined or assumed to be Mexico City, where she never had been. It was the number 4 bus on the Red Line, driving past a large park at night. Strings of yellow lanterns were hung along the border of the park. The air was misting heavily. Shadows moved behind the lanterns, irregular shapes that Ava, watching from her seat next to a window on the bus, could not properly discern or identify.

Suddenly the doors flew open. Many small dark men invaded the bus, all of them dressed in black and wearing the woolen hats of mountain people. They spoke rapidly to each other in a dialect Ava did not understand and sat in the aisle rather than on the seats. There were so many men that they stumbled over each other and fell, eliciting shouts and cries of displeasure.

Ava sat as close to the window as she could, not wanting to get in their way or come into contact with the men and have them fall on her. In this dream she was a young girl, perhaps nine or ten years old. She looked back at the lanterns lining the park. They were blue and the bus was passing a different landscape. Ava realized that the men must have jumped aboard the bus as it was moving. Then she saw her mother sitting alone in a donkey cart at the side of the road. The donkey was lying on the ground, still in harness, but it appeared to have collapsed and died, its legs sticking out at awkward angles.

"Mamacita! Mamacita!" the young Ava cried. She tried to open the window but it wouldn't budge. The bus rumbled by the cart attached to the prostrate beast. Ava became hysterical; she wanted her mother. The girl got up from her seat and stepped on the men, desperate to escape from the bus. The little men did not pay any attention to Ava as she climbed over them. They continued to talk rapidly in their incomprehensible language, oblivious to her concerns. She banged on the rear door, imploring the driver—if there was one—to stop and allow her to disembark.

Finally the door came away. It did not open—it fell off, or disappeared as if it were never there. Ava found herself alone, standing at the edge of a body of black water. She could see lights shimmering across the pond, the yellow lanterns of the park. Ava had to find her mother and she set out to walk around the pond, heading in the direction she thought would be the quickest route to the donkey cart.

Ten steps later Ava was waist-deep in the water. She couldn't move. She felt as if the lower half of her body was gone, swallowed by the blackness. Ava tried to scream but there seemed to be an object in her throat that prevented the issue of any noise. She began to gag and cough in an effort to expel the obstruction. The water turned from black to red. Ava the child was drowning in blood.

She awoke gasping for air, her eyes filled with tears. Ava wiped them away and steadied her breathing. She heard a scraping sound from above and looked up at the ceiling. A small dark brown bat depended from the molding.

DELRAY'S DREAM

DELRAY DECIDED to take a nap before going to meet Ava. He drank three beers and after finishing off the last one peeked out into the hallway to see if Framboyán Lanzar's body was still there. It was. He closed the door, stumbled over to the bed, lay down, and immediately fell asleep.

DelRay dreamed that he and his father, who appeared to be only slightly older than DelRay was now (and was also in the dream), were walking together on a narrow path through a jungle inhabited by marvelous songbirds. Duro was enchanted by the music and stepped quickly ahead, forcing his son to hurry in order to stay with him. Duro plunged deeper into the leafy bush. DelRay struggled to keep up. Exquisitely colored birds flashed before, above, and by them. DelRay had never seen such bright reds, yellows, greens, and blues. Their brilliance blinded him and he was forced to stop and close his eyes. When DelRay reopened them and looked around, Duro was gone.

DelRay shouted out to his father but the only response came from the birds. He staggered forward, fighting against the thick, reaching foliage. DelRay soon grew weary and sat down on the ground to rest. An orange-and-white-striped viper appeared before him, waving its triangular head and flicking a forked purple tongue. DelRay noticed that the snake had no eyes. He reached out his right hand and caressed the serpent, which wound itself around DelRay's wrist. Duro exploded out of the forest with a machete and with one swipe severed his son's right arm.

DelRay awoke covered with sweat. He got up and opened the door to the corridor. Framboyán's body was gone.

BELIEVERS

INDIO DESACATO delicately fingered the thick bandage on his neck. The wrapping restricted his movements and he had to turn his entire body in order to pick up and speak into his office telephone.

"Talk."

"Boss, it's me. Thankful."

"Where are you?"

"Big D. Pickin' up the Eyetalian girl. You asked me to, remember?"

"Oh, yeah. Since I got shot I ain't been thinkin' straight."

"I was sorry to hear about it, *jefe*. Can't go anyplace these days somebody don't pop somebody. How you feelin'?"

"Better than La Viuda. She don't feel nothin'. I saw the *nagual*, amigo. Stared into his evil eyes and lived to tell about it. Countin' my blessings. When does her plane get in?"

"Delayed. Bad weather in Milan. Gonna be three hours late. I'll get us a hotel room, come back tomorrow."

"*Two* rooms, Priest. This is expensive merch."

"I wasn't gonna touch her, boss. Just thought it'd be better, one room. Keep an eye on her she tries to run."

"You only *got* one eye, *chico*. You want to keep it, keep your hands off the merch."

"Of course, boss, of course. Never had a nasty thought."

"Every man makes nasty, Thankful, they get the opportunity. The Lord's brother, James, said, 'Every man is tempted, when he is drawn away of his own lust, and enticed. Then when lust hath conceived, it bringeth forth sin: and sin, when it is finished, bringeth forth death.' "

"I hear you."

"Sure you do. *Hasta mañana.*"

"See you then, boss, with the goods."

Indio hung up. The phone rang again. Indio's hand was still on it.

"Talk."

"Hello, Indio. It's Sonny."

"Sonny, where you at?"

"Vegas. I'm leavin' tonight for Houston, so I'll see you tomorrow evening, as planned."

"I'm looking forward to it. Will Emilio be coming?"

"I'm afraid not. He has a situation in Detroit. I heard you had a scrape in Old Mexico. You okay?"

Indio patted the bandage on his neck and shoulder. "Yeah, I'll live."

"Girls and guns has never been a winning combination."

"Sonny, I'm a believer."

"I ever tell ya about Sheila, my second wife, who she woke me up with the nose of a forty-five on the head of my dick?"

"No."

"She had found out I was bangin' LaMona, who become my third wife after. Threatened to blow away my cock I didn't stop."

"Sonny, Jesus."

"Swore on my grandmother Natalie's grave I would. Soon as she eased off the hammer I punched her in the nose. Funny thing, LaMona's the one actually shot me. In the right foot."

"Your third wife?"

"Yeah. Found out I was bangin' Penny Annie, who was dancin' at Caesar's then."

"You marry her?"

"Who? Penny Annie?"

"Yeah."

"No. I woulda, too, but she got whacked with Ralphie the Rumanian on his yacht."

"Oh, yeah. The Saigon setup."

"Probably for the best. I didn't marry her, I mean. Women and me, I don't know. We don't do too good the distance. See you tomorrow, Indio."

"*Hasta*, Sonny."

THE ONE-EYED LIZARD

DELRAY DECIDED to fortify himself before going to La Casa Desacato at midnight. He drove out the opposite end of town from El Oráculo and stopped at a bar named El Lagarto Tuerto. Mudo's left bootheel hit the sand just as a corona discharge gyrated onto a telephone pole next to the highway. DelRay ducked back into his Cutlass as he watched St. Elmo's fire roll along the line like an acrobat riding a bicycle on a high wire. The blue-white lightning ball danced daintily on its silent path for several seconds, then disappeared as rapidly as it had come, leaving only a patch of mist in its wake. There had been no thunder or noise other than a faint hiss following the sphere's decay.

DelRay waited a few moments before again attempting to disembark. He recalled having read in *UFO Monthly*, one of the waiting-room magazines at Chifla Miguel's that DelRay and the other mechanics occasionally perused during lunch breaks, that ball lightning was often misidentified as a spaceship. In fact it was gas or air behaving in an unusual way, powered perhaps by a high-frequency electromagnetic field or focused cosmic ray particles. As he lowered his leg again to the ground, DelRay heard thunder, and he hurried toward the bar before the rain came. Thunderstorms, he knew, functioned as batteries to keep the earth charged negatively and the atmosphere charged positively.

DelRay reached the entrance just as several tons of water hit the earth in his immediate vicinity. As far as it being a good or bad omen, he couldn't tell. DelRay only hoped that God knew what He was doing, because he wasn't so sure about about himself.

There were only two customers inside, both seated on bar stools, since there were no tables or chairs. DelRay stood at the bar for two minutes but no bartender appeared. He turned to the patron nearest him and was about to ask if someone were working, but the man was sound asleep, snoring with his head resting on his arms on the counter. DelRay shifted his attention to a black-bearded man at the opposite end who sat staring at the label of a beer bottle in front of him.

"Hey, pardner," DelRay said, "anybody serving?"

The man did not respond.

"Hey, buddy. Amigo! I asked, anybody work here?"

The customer so addressed promptly fell off of his bar stool, out of DelRay's sight.

"Jesus, what a place," said Mudo.

He could hear the storm raging outside, loud thunder and heavy rain. Nevertheless DelRay turned toward the door.

"Welcome to the One-Eyed Lizard!" boomed a voice behind him.

Mudo did a one-eighty and saw a white-haired woman who stood well over six feet tall. She had a hawk nose and eyes that went with it. The woman was wearing a checkered shirt and blue jeans held up by red suspenders spread wide by her enormous bosom. DelRay pegged her age at fifty-five, give or take a few.

"You want a drink or not?" she barked.

DelRay returned to the bar. "I didn't see anybody workin'."

"You see someone now, don't ya?"

"I certainly do."

"What'll it be?"

"Lone Star, I guess."

The large woman squinted, taking a closer look at him.

"You're a cloudy boy, all right."

"Cloudy?"

"Not too certain about yourself."

She produced a bottle of beer, cracked it open and placed it on the bar in front of DelRay, where it foamed over onto the counter.

"How can you tell?" he asked.

The woman snorted. "There's even more I can't —*won't*—tell ya. I've got the gift."

"The gift?"

"The gift of seein' both the present and the future at the same time. See my eyes?"

DelRay stared at them. Both were pale blue with extraordinarily dilated pupils.

"A seer, son. Same as Amos, Asaph, Gad, Heman, Samuel and Zadok. You heard of them, ain't ya?"

"No, ma'am."

"Where was you brought up, boy?"

"Arizona."

She stared directly at DelRay, leaning forward, her large hands pressing down hard on the bar. Her right eye wandered, jerked, rolled around. DelRay watched it move.

"Your right eye the one sees the future?"

The woman leaned back. Her eye calmed down.

"Break thou the arm of the wicked and the evil man," she said. "Seek out his wickedness till thou find none."

DelRay said, "You mean Indio?"

"Drink up and go."

He took a long swig from the bottle, set it back down on the counter, and pulled a dollar from his pocket.

"No charge," the woman said. "Go your way. I send you forth as a lamb among wolves."

DelRay ran through the rain to his car, got in and sat there thinking about what the woman had said. Suddenly, a single vertical bolt of cloud-to-ground lightning exited as a bright pink spot atop the thunderhead. It struck the tin roof of El Lagarto Tuerto and ignited the Cutlass's engine. DelRay sat in the idling automobile, trembling. His cock twitched, and he realized he had an erection.

THE GREAT HEAT

BY THE TIME DelRay arrived at La Casa Desacato it was ten past midnight. He had never been inside before, so he didn't know what to expect. At the door he was greeted by a small Mexican woman of late middle age, wearing a plain black dress, a white gardenia held in her gray-black hair by a red comb. Her pleasantly wrinkled face was relaxed except for the eyes, the gleaming intensity of which spooked DelRay.

"May I help you?" she asked.

"I want your most expensive girl. I have money." He slurred his words, pretending to be slightly drunk.

The woman let him in. "Wait here," she said,

motioning to an array of comfortable-looking chairs, then left DelRay alone in the dimly lit front room.

He stood, wondering where everybody was, why there was no noise. One minute later Ava appeared, alone, draped in a short, pink robe.

"Hello, chico," she said. "My name is Ava."

She took his arm and escorted him down a long corridor to a bedroom. They went in and Ava closed the door behind them.

"Jesus, Ava. . . ."

She kissed DelRay hard. His mouth hurt. Ava took his hands and placed them on her tits, pressing herself against him.

"Let's fuck before we kill him," she said, shedding the robe, which was all she had on.

Her face looked different to DelRay. He didn't move.

"Come on, Del. Let's do it."

Ava moved to the bed, knelt on it, and held out her left hand to him. DelRay took off his shoes and pants and went to her. Ava lay down and spread her legs.

"I need you, Del. I really do."

Ava reached down for his cock. It was soft. She stroked him gently at first, then stronger as his blood rose. When he was hard enough, she guided him into her.

"Fuck me, Del! Fuck me hard! Fast, do it fast!"

DelRay drove his body against Ava's. He felt the great heat coming from her and did his best, but it wasn't what he wanted. What he wanted didn't matter to Ava, however. She used his cock for her own purposes, paying no attention to him. This was an Ava DelRay had never been with before. She shoved herself forward and grunted, over and over. DelRay held his body stiff and straight, letting her thrust. He watched her face go almost black, her eyes closed. They flashed open for a second, reminding him of a wild horse. She tossed her black mane across her face. Del slid forward, penetrating Ava as deeply as he could, pushing and being pushed back until he felt her cunt contract and the muscles flutter. Ava gripped his back and sides with her arms and legs as tightly as she could, then released him, and herself.

"You didn't come, did you, Del?"

"No."

Ava laughed. "I guess I owe you one."

DelRay rolled off of Ava onto his back.

"What about Indio?" he said.

"He's asleep in his bedroom. He got shot up a

little in Mexico. We're gonna shoot him up some more. You ready?"

DelRay's cock bent stiffly against his belly. Ava got on her knees, then lowered her head over him.

"I'll take care of this first," she said. "Then we'll really get down to business."

RIFIF

"MOST OF THE GIRLS are at a private party tonight," Ava told DelRay. "At a ranch outside of town. That's why it's so quiet."

Ava wore jeans, boots and a cowboy shirt. Around her neck she'd wound the green scarf with parrots on it that DelRay had bought for her in Nogales. She had two guns, nine-millimeter Sig Sauers, one of which she handed to DelRay.

"Where did you get these?"

"From a client. An arms dealer from Zip City, Alabama, named Farfel El Perro."

"How did you pay for them?"

"You really want to know?"

"Yeah."

"I let him in the back door without a raincoat. It's the easiest way to get AIDS, but I figured I'd take the chance for *la causa.*"

"*La causa?*"

Ava kissed him quickly on the lips. "*Vámonos,* baby. We've only got a small window of time."

DelRay followed her down the corridor, then along another until they came to rosewood double doors at what DelRay guessed was the far end of the house. Ava fished a key out of a pocket of her jeans and inserted it into the lock. She turned it slowly until they both heard a click, and Ava opened one of the doors.

Indio was sound asleep in the fetal position on his canopied four-poster bed. The couple crept up to him and Ava placed the nose of her gun against the pimp's exposed right ear.

"Time to rise, Desacato," she said.

He stirred. One eye opened.

"Easy now," said Ava. "No fast moves. Get up slowly."

Indio followed orders. He slid off the bed and stood next to it in his blue silk pajamas and fresh bandages.

"Push the bed aside, Del," she said.

"You don't want to do this, Ava," said Indio.

DelRay moved the bed and pulled away an oriental throw rug that had been under it, revealing a floor safe. He read the gold lettering on the black steel: HERRING-HALL MARVIN SAFE CO. SAN FRANCISCO.

"Open it," Ava told Indio, holding her Sig Sauer against his right cheek.

"You and your boyfriend are already dead."

"Open it."

Indio knelt down, spun the combination, and pulled the heavy lever.

"Stand up," Ava said. "Move away from there."

Indio stood and moved. She kept him covered.

"Take a look, Del. There's probably a gun."

DelRay stuck his nine-millimeter into his pants and bent to it. He reached in and pulled up an ugly hunk of metal.

"Big sucker. Weaver .300 H&H magnum."

"We'll take it with us. Is the money there?"

DelRay set the gun down on the floor and unearthed a large canvas sack. He opened it and peered inside.

"Christ, Ava. It must be a million bucks in here."

"Half a million," she said. "Right, Indio?"

The pimp kept silent.

"Hand me a pillow, Del."

He got up, took one off the bed and gave it to her.

"Put the Weaver in the sack and close it up."

DelRay did as she commanded.

"Get down on your knees," she told Indio. "Hold this pillow over your face."

The pimp took the pillow from her and held it.

"You're a whore from hell," he said.

"Stick your fucking face in the pillow."

As Indio's nose pressed satin, Ava shoved the barrel of her Sig Sauer into it and fired. The pimp jumped back a foot and collapsed on his left side. Blood gushed from what formerly had been his forehead. Ava picked up the pillow and placed it over Desacato's face.

Ava and DelRay walked out of the house with the money.

"Head south," Ava ordered DelRay as they climbed into the Cutlass. The sack was in the trunk.

DelRay drove south out of town. After they had gone ten miles, Ava said, "Pull over here."

Mudo eased the Cutlass to a stop next to the highway. He saw another car parked a short distance away. It looked like an '86 Thunderbird. DelRay turned toward

Ava and saw that she had her pistol pointed at him.

"Give me your gun," she said.

"Ava, what the hell?"

"I don't want to shoot you, Del. I really don't. Give it to me."

He gave up the Sig Sauer.

"Now, get out of the car. Slowly."

DelRay opened the driver's side door and got out. Ava slid across the seat, taking the keys out of the ignition. She got out and stood next to him.

"Move," she said, motioning toward the rear of the car. She handed him the keys. "Open the trunk."

DelRay took the keys and unlocked it.

"Take out the bag and put it on the ground."

He did what she said.

"Get in."

"Ava. . . ."

"Get in, Del. Don't argue or I'll kill you, too."

DelRay climbed into the trunk. Ava tossed him the keys and closed the lid. He heard her dragging the sack; faintly, two doors slamming shut in succession; a car's ignition; wheels scraping purchase on dirt; then, nothing.

Twenty-five minutes before, DelRay thought, Ava had been sucking his cock.

NOCTURNAL
ADMISSION

"YOU SPEAK good English."

"I went to a British boarding school."

"You went to a boarding school in England?"

"Uh-huh."

"Then how...I mean...."

"How'd I become a hooker? Is that your question?"

Thankful Priest had picked up Carla Coltello at DFW and was driving to their hotel in Dallas. Flown in at Sonny "Mr. Nice" Cicatrice's expense, Carla Coltello was an internationally renowned prostitute whose customers included some of the world's wealthiest and most famous men—industrialists, actors, mob bosses. Sonny had met her in Taormina, where he had been on holiday six weeks before. Carla was with Vincenzo Troppofresco, the fashion designer, staying at the same hotel. She had given Sonny her card, he'd called, and now he was looking forward to two days of carnal delights, damn the expense. Carla was twenty-two years old, a quarter-inch under six feet tall, with a face like the young Elsa Martinelli's and a figure every bit as spectacular as Sophia Loren's at the same age. Thankful got a hard-on as soon as he saw her. He still had one.

"When I was seventeen," Carla told him, "a man—a friend of my father's—offered me a million lire to take off my clothes and pose for him while he masturbated."

"Did you do it?"

"Of course. That started me on my road toward financial independence. In two years, thanks to wise investments, I will be able to retire."

"Then what?"

"I will become a veterinarian and care for animals. That has always been my dream. And I will marry a very rich man, of course. Mine is a classic tale."

They checked into the hotel, where Carla went immediately to her room to sleep. Thankful was restless, so he went to the hotel bar. Without trying, Carla Coltello had turned him on big time, and he needed to cool down before attempting to crash. As he got older, Thankful found that he required less and less sleep, anyway. The bar was practically empty. Priest ordered a double Johnnie Walker Black on the rocks. Forty-five minutes and four double scotches later, Thankful was, as Indio would put it, "tighter than the Flyin' fuckin' Nun's pussy." He couldn't get Carla out of his mind or rid himself of the super erection she had inspired. The Cyclopean henchman knew he had to take a shot at her.

Thankful knocked on Carla's door. She responded after his fifth attempt.

"What is it?" she asked from behind the closed door.

"It's me, Thankful Priest. I want to talk to you."

"Really, Mr. Priest, I must sleep. I'm sure you could use some yourself."

"That's not what I had in mind to use."

"I figured as much. Wait a minute."

Thankful leaned against the door. A few seconds later a piece of paper slid under the door into the hallway.

He bent down and picked it up. "What's this?"

"Look at it," said Carla.

Thankful turned the piece of paper over and saw that it was a nude photograph of Carla Coltello. In the picture she was seated on a white chair on a sunny terrace, biting into a red apple.

"This is you," said Thankful.

"Full frontal nudity," said Carla. "Use it well. But do me a favor."

"What's that?"

"Wait until you get back to your room. 'Night."

Thankful Priest lingered for a moment, studying the photo in the dim hallway light. His eye was not focusing correctly. Carla's magnificent breasts appeared to have smiling faces drawn on them. Thankful smiled back.

DESERT TIME

BY THE TIME Mr. Nice arrived at La Casa Desacato, Thankful had removed Indio's body and had it chauffeured to Sparky and Buddy's Funeral Parlor. Carla was ensconced in one of the rooms, but once he learned of Indio's murder and the robbery Sonny was no longer in a mood to dally. He made a few phone calls, then ordered Thankful to make arrangements for Carla Coltello's return to Italy. He didn't even want to see her. The thought of losing so much money made him physically ill. Being done out of money, Sonny believed, was the only thing in the world worse than becoming impotent. He handed Thankful an envelope to give to Carla and told him to send into

Desacato's office, which Cicatrice had commandeered, Señora Matrera, the whore wrangler who had admitted the man who assisted Ava Varazo. Señora Matrera described DelRay Mudo to Mr. Nice as best she could, and explained that the house was almost empty when the crime took place. She had not even heard a shot.

DelRay had managed to extricate himself from the car trunk by prying apart the lock with a tire tool. He knew he couldn't stick around Sinaloa, but he wasn't certain where to go. Before getting into the driver's seat of his Cutlass, DelRay stood by the side of the road in the desert and cursed himself for his stupidity. He had realized while imprisoned in the trunk that it was Ava who had murdered Framboyán Lanzar. A stiff wind blew sand in his face, stinging his eyes and lips, infesting his hair.

DelRay remembered a scene from a movie he had watched on TV in the trailer home of Churro Muchaco, a mechanic friend of his back in Arizona. In the film a woman who has double-crossed one man and run off with another, leaving the first sucker holding the bag for a crime she had committed, says to her new twist, "It don't pay to depend on anybody else, does it, Eddie? I mean, men and women, we was born to disappoint each other."

"Bitch got that right," Churro Muchaco had said. "Dude gonna play that game, he best show up *correct!*"

Standing alone in the cruel nightwind, DelRay knew Churro would rag him righteously for allowing Ava Varazo to make a fool of him. He had never felt more incorrect in his life.

PART TWO

LA VILLANÍA

COBRA AND LEANDER

LEANDER RAY "Lee" Rhodes was born in Bad Leopard, Idaho, on January 20, 1937. His parents, Ardmore and Feline Law Rhodes, at that time owned and operated a small grocery store and the local branch of the United States Post Office. The population of Bad Leopard to this day has never exceeded 108. In 1937 there were fewer than fifty permanent residents. Ardmore Rhodes had been a professor of Obscure Religions at UCLA until 1930, when he decided that human beings were God's failed experiments, their imperfections increasing geometrically by generations, and that he would be better off far away from most of them.

Ardmore and his then-girlfriend Feline Law, the daughter of a gardener at Pickfair whom he had met on a rainy Sunday afternoon on the Santa Monica pier, where each of them had gone to be alone, left Los Angeles together without telling anyone. They drove Ardmore's Ford to Reno, Nevada, where they were married. The Justice of the Peace who performed the ceremony told the newlyweds over coffee and doughnuts that he had recently returned from a fishing trip on the Big Bad Leopard River in Idaho. He informed them that he had not seen another human being for ten full days. Thirty minutes later Ardmore and Feline were headed that way.

Leander was an only child and something of an accident at that. His parents practiced coitus interruptus in the hope of never conceiving a child, and they were successful for almost seven years. When Leander Ray arrived, however, his parents were not at all displeased. The boy, they decided, would be their experiment in perfectibility. It was their hope that Leander Ray Rhodes would turn out to be a very special person.

The young Leander did not disappoint, proving adept as a woodsman, hunter, and fly fisherman; and his talents in the sciences and study of literature earned him numerous scholastic awards. When he joined the Marine Corps on the eve of his scheduled departure to begin his freshman year at the Massachusetts Institute of Technology, Ardmore and Feline were not entirely surprised or disappointed. Since the age of sixteen Leander Ray had become increasingly preoccupied with military history. His recreational reading almost exclusively concerned battle strategy; Lee's bedside books during his junior and senior years of high school were Clausewitz's *On War* and Ulmer von Umleitung's *Militärische Technik*.

After leaving Bad Leopard, Idaho, for boot camp, Lee Rhodes returned only once, for the double funeral of Ardmore and Feline. His parents had committed suicide together while Lee was serving his second tour in Vietnam as a military advisor. Feline and Ardmore had set fire to their house and allowed the flames to consume them and all of their possessions. They left behind only a note to Lee, tacked to the wooden gate at the entrance to their property: "Son, now nobody can ever disturb us. We know you will understand."

Following a twenty-year stretch as a Marine, Leander Ray retired from the service with the rank of lieutenant colonel. He went to New Orleans, where he lived in a rented room on Lafreniere Street in the seventh ward and collected his pension while indulging himself in an intense study of the works of Louis-Ferdinand Céline, Julien Gracq, and Junichiro Tanizaki. Lee chose New Orleans based on a brief friendship he had had with a black lieutenant named Ivory Coates, who had been a native of that city. Ivory Coates was killed during the Tet Offensive but before his death he told Leander Ray about New Orleans and his life there prior to joining the Marine Corps. Lee appreciated the passionate affection with which Ivory had described his home place, so he decided to see if it would suit him, too.

In N.O., Leander Ray met a young African-American woman named Cobra Box, a resident of the Reincarnation public housing project, where she lived with her mother and brother. Cobra was seventeen and a half years old and worked as a maid at the Monteleone Hotel on Royal. Lee noticed Cobra on Canal Street, waiting for a bus after work. Struck by Cobra's ebony beauty, her regal posture, Leander Ray introduced himself and invited the girl to have dinner with him that very evening. She declined, not altogether politely, and boarded the next bus.

Unable to dismiss her from his mind, Lee returned to the same bus stop each afternoon for a week at approximately the same time, repeating his invitation to Cobra Box until finally, on his fifth attempt, she agreed to accompany him to the Hidden Pearl Chinese restaurant on St. Charles for a cup of tea.

Cobra's mother, Yarvella, Lee learned, was originally from Bogue Chitto, Mississippi; she, too, worked as a maid, at a Holiday Inn near the airport. Cobra's brother, Fidel, her twin, was a member of a gang called Dead Menz Eyz that terrorized the other residents of Reincarnation. Leander Ray had read about them in the newspaper and heard about their alleged drug dealing and other crime-related activities virtually nightly on the TV news. Cobra confessed to Lee that she did not expect Fidel would live to celebrate his eighteenth birthday. Lee continued to meet Cobra at the bus stop almost every day, and most of the time she would go with him for tea or coffee. Then one day he got on the bus and rode with her to Reincarnation.

Cobra was impressed by Leander Ray's intrepid demeanor; being the only white person at the project did not seem to disturb or intimidate him at all. Lee made a similarly good impression on Yarvella, who, though she was suspicious of his motives at first, was soon won over by Lee's straightforward manner. She was not displeased as Leander Ray became a regular visitor to the Box home. It was not until his fourth time there that he encountered Fidel. Confrontational at first, Fidel softened when Lee engaged him in a conversation about weapons.

Within a month Lee asked Cobra to marry him, and she accepted. Yarvella did not object. The retired lieutenant colonel convinced Fidel to join the Marine Corps, a move Leander Ray helped to facilitate. Since the sudden, violent death by stabbing of the twins' father, Ferdinand Magellan Box, shortly after their sixth birthday, they had had no paternal input, and Yarvella welcomed Leander Ray's advice and guidance.

Cobra quit her job at the Monteleone and devoted her time to Lee. He, in turn, devoted himself to Cobra, tutoring her in the arts and sciences. Lee also helped to support Yarvella, which was easy to do thanks to his pension and modest lifestyle. On Cobra's twenty-first birthday Yarvella received via special messenger a letter from Leander Ray and Cobra informing her that henceforth Lee's Marine Corps pension would be coming to Yarvella in full every month, and that they had already departed New Orleans. Lee had decided to take a position of a military nature in another country, he explained, and for the very best of reasons:

to assist people in their struggle for freedom. Cobra had agreed to accompany and support him on this mission. Leander Ray and Cobra Box Rhodes ended their letter to her mother with the words, "We know you will understand."

BAD HEAD

LEANDER RAY'S friend Asa Hand, with whom he had bunked at Parris Island, fought beside in Nam, on Grenada, in El Salvador and beaten like a rug at poker and blackjack for the better part of two decades, had written to Lee from Mexico, imploring him to join in "a good fight for a change. Got my head bad down here one too many times, I guess," Asa Hand wrote. "Woke up one day and what I saw wasn't poverty, it was misery. Only so many beatings, jailings, tortures and assassinations a man can ignore, along with the low pay, pisspoor working conditions, land ripoffs, exploitation of the general population by oil and drug cartels, etc., before he decides to get off his pimply butt and do something. One statistic: Last year 17,000 Indians died of hunger. Lee, it's acceptable for people to die of cancer, of AIDS, of heartbreak. But hunger? The caciques are selling off the peasants' land the campesino cooperatives granted them after the revolution of 1910. This ain't communism versus capitalism, good buddy, it's life or death. Two-thirds of the people here in La Villanía, where I'm headquartered, have no electricity, they live in dirt-floor huts. At the Ejido Santa Maria Luisa, kids eat every other day, adults twice a week. The irony is that the region is one of Mexico's richest, with hundreds of millions of dollars available for agricultural development and petroleum research and drilling. Trouble is that only 15 to 20% of that money has actually been spent—the rest is in the pockets and bank accounts of a small group of people who maintain control over politics by keeping the state backwards. Sound familiar? Come on down, man. The Indians call me a tatic, an honored one. You can be a tatic, too. These people need us, Lee. This is the final nail in their coffin. Mexico is on the verge of becoming one big maquiladora. Come on down and lend a Hand a hand."

Leander Ray showed Cobra Asa Hand's letter and told her he had to go. She read it and said she understood but that he had to take her with him.

"You don't," said Cobra Box, "you might wake up with more than a bad head go along with the parts be missin'."

Lee grinned, embraced his wife, and said, "Cobra, I truly wish my folks could have met you. You're their kind of people."

"What does La Villanía mean?"

"Nasty."

Cobra laughed.

"What's so funny?"

"Baby," Cobra said, "I believe I been there before."

THE RED SCORPION

DelRay ARRIVED in La Villanía at dusk. He slowed down the mud-encrusted Cutlass and idled alongside an old man leading a donkey by a piece of rope. A large sack was slung across the donkey's back.

"Pardon me, mister, but I'm looking for Ava Varazo. Do you know where she lives?"

The old man kept walking ahead of the donkey. He pointed in the direction he was going.

"The house with a blue roof," he said.

"*Gracias.*"

DelRay drove forward and parked next to the house to which he had been directed. He killed the engine and climbed out. A rough wind blew dirt into

his eyes and Mudo wiped it away. He looked down
at the red ground, blinked several times, then looked
up and saw her. Ava was wearing a white dress, and
her long black hair was tied straight back. She wore
no makeup.

"You're either smarter than I thought," she said,
"or dumber. Which is it?"

"I got more questions now than I can handle."

"I'll tell you one thing."

"What's that?"

"I'm not the same woman here that I was across
the border."

DelRay took a good look at her. Aside from her
simple clothes, hair and undecorated face, Ava seemed
more robust than she had in Texas; but the real difference was in her eyes. They were the 8-balls of a
hawk confronting its prey. DelRay searched them for
a speck of charity. She held a revolver in her right
hand, the barrel pointed at the ground.

"You left me in a pretty tough spot, Ava. You ran
out on me."

"There is a war going on here, Del. If you want
to fight with us, you can stay."

"What if I just want my share of the money?"

"The money was used for guns and ammunition."

"I don't know why, Ava, but it's good to see you."

Ava's eyes brightened, then softened slightly. She smiled. "Come in and eat."

The old man came by, leading the donkey. He looked at Ava.

"Hello, Javier," she said, then turned toward the house.

DelRay watched the old man pass. He noticed that a human hand was hanging from one end of the bundle balanced on the donkey's back. A large red scorpion perched perfectly still in a fold of the sack.

"Come on, Del," said Ava.

He followed her.

THE CHANCE
OF A LIFETIME

"CAN'T UNDERSTAND how Indio let that broad get the drop on him."

"He was a good man to work for. I'm gonna miss him."

Thankful Priest and Sonny "Mr. Nice" Cicatrice were cruising south on Texas State Highway 277 in Indio Desacato's Lincoln Mark VIII. Thankful was at the wheel. They were passing through Val Verde County and had just crossed Dry Devils, headed for Del Rio and the plunge into Old Mexico. Thankful Priest had telephoned Puma Charlie in La Paz, Arizona, and Charlie told him that Ava Varazo was from La Villanía, Mexico. Other than that, Puma

Charlie said, he didn't really know a whole hell of a lot about her. Sonny insisted that since they had nothing else to go on, La Villanía was as good a place as any to begin the trackdown. If she had any family left down there, he reasoned, they might know where she was.

Thankful had shut down the house in Sinaloa for the time being, leaving Señora Matrera and Moke Lamer as caretakers until he returned. The girls had been given a holiday and told to contact Señora Matrera in two weeks. Indio's corpse was cremated, which had been his desire, and his ashes scattered by Moke Lamer into the languid, rust-colored creek called Río Pestoso, with Thankful and Señora Matrera in attendance. Moke then played "La Golondrina," Indio's favorite tune, on a guitar, after which Thankful fired into the air a single round from his fallen *jefe's* Glock pistol, and tossed the gun into the foul water. *"¡Un fuerte abrazo, amigo!"* Priest shouted, and the ceremony was over.

"After we get the money," Sonny said, "we kill her and whoever else is around. Agreed?"

Thankful nodded. "I go with you, *jefe!*"

"What's that?"

"Means I agree."

"Good. You know why I got the name Mr. Nice?"

"No."

"Tommaso 'Short Hair' Fabregas, remember him?"

"Uh-uh."

"An independent out of Tampa. Knocked off a casino on Paradise Island, the Bahamas. Big Tony sent me to find him. I was nineteen years old, never killed nobody. Caught up with Short Hair in New Orleans. Suite 1515, DeSalvo Hotel. I'll never forget it. He's in there with his wife. I confront Tommaso, tell him Big Tony don't want the money back. He asks me what then? Short Hair's on his knees. I got a hair-trigger .45 kissed to his forehead. His balls, I say. Tony wants the major stones he must have to done what he did. Tommaso tries to make a deal. I decline. He says okay, kill me, but don't touch my wife."

"What's she doin'?"

"Sittin' on the couch. Doesn't say a word."

"What'd you do?"

"I shot him. Just once. The bullet completely penetrated the skull, come out the back of his head. The wife don't peep. I took out a ten-inch blade I had in my pocket and gave it to her. Told her cut off her husband's balls."

"Christ, Sonny. She did this?"

"Gets down next to him, pulls down his pants. You know what she says?"

"What?"

" 'Should I cut off his dick, too?' "

Thankful almost lost control of the car. "No!" he shouted.

"Exactly the words. I said no, just the nuts. She handles the knife like a brain surgeon. I give her a plastic bag I had for the purpose. She sticks 'em in there, hands it to me. She wipes the blade clean on Short Hair's shirt, folds it, gives it back. Now guess what she says."

"Tell me."

" 'You'll be nice, won't you?' That's what she says. I say whattaya mean, be nice? Tommaso's request, she reminds me. He asked that I don't touch her. I say sure, I'll be nice, I ain't an animal. She's there on her knees. Before she can stand I shoot her right between the eyes, same as her bandit husband. Didn't touch her."

"Mr. Nice."

Sonny laughed. "Big Tony wanted to know the details when I bring him Short Hair Fabregas's balls. He hung the name on me."

"Was she good lookin'?"

"Who? The wife?"

"Yeah."

"Not particularly I can recall. Why?"

"Just wonderin' what kind of woman would do that, slice off her old man's nuts."

"She would've cut his cock, too. It was her chance of a lifetime, Priest, every broad's dream. I was really nice, I'd have let her."

LAND OF THE PANDAS

"**YOU EVER HEAR** of Julia Pastrana?"

"No, who's she?"

"Was. The Wolfwoman of Mexico."

Ava Varazo and Cobra Box were sitting together on cane chairs in front of Ava's house, smoking cigarettes, at one o'clock in the morning. Darkness did nothing to mitigate against the fiery air. DelRay Mudo, Lee Rhodes, and Asa Hand were inside the house, manufacturing reloads.

"*Wolf*woman?"

"Uh-huh," said Ava. "A hundred-fifty years ago, I guess, she was born near here with long, thick black hair all over her face and body. Julia Pastrana, called the Wolfwoman. Most famous person from this part of the country. A man named Theodore Lent spotted her in a Yucatán circus sideshow, married her and became her manager. They toured all over Europe and the United States. He made a fortune."

"Bet he beat on her."

"Probably. She was his meal ticket, that's for sure. Even after she died."

"What he do then?"

"Sold her corpse to a Russian anatomist who mummified her. Somehow, a few years later, Lent got it back and exhibited Julia's mummy."

"Where is it now?"

"In Norway. The Wolfwoman was supposedly lost for a century, then in 1990 it turned up at the Oslo Forensic Institute. The anthropology museum in Mexico City is trying to reclaim her for our own country. There's even an organization called Amigas de Julia Pastrana."

"Conditions never been very good for any kinds of women anywhere, with hair or without."

"That's one of the things we're fighting for."

"I tell you, Ava, I'd like to go to China someday, live in the Land of the Pandas."

"What's that?"

"Chinese government preserved one million acres just for pandas to roam around in. The panda is my favorite animal."

"The Chinese people get hungry enough," Ava said, "they'll eat those pandas."

Cobra dropped her cigarette butt in the dust and closed her eyes. She imagined herself walking naked through a cool bamboo forest, surrounded by hundreds of hidden pandas. Julia Pastrana could have lived among the pandas in her middle and old age, Cobra thought, after patches of her body hair had turned white and she looked more like a panda than a wolf.

PAYBACK

THE REVOLUTIONARY movement was called Las Gotas de Lluvia Incontables (GLI), "The Countless Raindrops." The rebels believed themselves to be as unstoppable as rain. They were engaged in what they termed a prodemocracy war, a just war, calling for the government to adhere to the principles upon which the Mexican constitution was founded. Asa Hand and other military experts had joined them in their struggle for liberty and equality because they were not merely a new version of the socialist and communist Third World guerrilla movements to which Latin America has long been accustomed. This was a legitimate revolution, a crusade that was steadily gaining support throughout the country.

When Sonny Cicatrice and Thankful Priest arrived in La Villanía in Indio Desacato's Lincoln Mark VIII, Leander Ray Rhodes and Asa Hand were ready for them. They figured correctly that if DelRay Mudo could find Ava Varazo so easily it was inevitable that the bad guys would not be far behind. By the time the Lincoln cruised one late afternoon through the village, the inhabitants had been alerted and knew what to do. A GLI lookout stationed close to the road two miles away had radioed to headquarters information about the approaching vehicle and the Raindrops had cleared the citizens off the streets.

"Where are the people?" asked Sonny. "You see anybody?"

"Maybe they're all taking a siesta," said Priest.

Thankful turned the big car down a side street, the unpaved surface of which was particularly rough —full of ruts and rocks, stressing the Lincoln's suspension system to the fullest.

"God damn it!" Sonny roared, as his head hit the roof. "Watch where you're going!"

"It's not my fault, Sonny. This is Mexico."

The car's right front tire hit a particularly deep pothole, causing the steering wheel to spin violently out of Thankful's control. He grasped desperately to regain his hold but at that point the sedan swiftly fishtailed. For an instant Priest thought they were about to roll over, but the impact killed the engine and the Lincoln quit in its tracks. The two men sat in the metal box enveloped in a swirling, blinding cloud of dust.

"Motherfuck!" yelled Mr. Nice.

When their visibility returned what Thankful and Sonny saw was nothing for which they were prepared. The car was surrounded by GLI guerrillas wearing camouflage fatigues and hooded black masks. Each of the dozen or so Raindrops wore a bandolier of bullets and held an M-16 rifle. Sonny pulled his .45-caliber Sig Sauer P-220 and exploded out the passenger side door.

"Sonny, no!" Thankful screamed.

By the time Mr. Nice squeezed the trigger, firing a few shells harmlessly into the air, he was dead. Four Raindrops had simultaneously ventilated the gangster at point-blank range. Thankful sat still behind the steering wheel, the palms of his hands pressing hard against the padding above his head.

"Get out!" ordered one of the soldiers.

The Cyclops complied, keeping his hands away from his body. He stood next to the car.

"Who are you? Why are you here?" asked the same soldier.

"My name is Thankful Priest. I'm looking for Ava Varazo."

"Why?"

"She has something that belongs to other people."

Thankful saw a red 1986 Thunderbird moving very slowly toward him from the opposite end of the street. It stopped approximately ten yards from where he stood. Priest tried to make out the faces of the driver and the passenger in the front seat, but the windshield was cracked and covered with a thick coat of dust, obscuring his vision. One of the soldiers came forward and poked the tip of a rifle against Thankful's chest. Priest looked into the soldier's eyes.

"Whore!" he said.

Ava pulled the trigger.

PART THREE

THE GOOD FIGHT

THE GREAT
WHITE NORTH

COBRA BOX LEFT Mexico carrying this shopping list:

—12 M-80s (light .30-caliber antitank guns)
—50 Lawes Rockets (collapsible, throwaway
  bazookas)
—6 Mortars with 100 rounds each
—2 cases of fragmentation grenades (50 per case)
—5,000 rounds of .225 ammo for M-16 rifles

She arrived in Idaho on her nineteenth birthday. Following the deaths of her husband, Leander Ray Rhodes, and his combat buddy Asa Hand by government troops in an ambush on the Río Jatate, just north of La Sultána in the Selva Lacandona, six months after

her arrival in Mexico, Cobra had remained with the
Countless Raindrops. In the company of Ava Varazo,
Cobra carried out night missions for the rebels while
residing with the Varazos in La Villanía.

DelRay Mudo had been given the assignment of
making contact with an underground weapons dealer
in Trouth City, Idaho, named Harmon White Bird.
Harmon White Bird was a quarter-blood Nez Perce
whom the GLI felt might be sympathetic to their
cause. DelRay had gone north three months before
Cobra Box headed after him. During that time there
had been no word from Mudo, and the Raindrops pre-
sumed he had defected or met with foul play.

Cobra bid a tearful farewell to Ava, with whom
she had developed a close friendship, and promised to
wire the code name PADRE LUNA to Ocosingo as
soon as she made contact with White Bird and delivered the order. The plan called for Ava Varazo to send
payment in cash dollars to Harmon White Bird via
private courier as soon as Cobra Box verified the deal.

Making her way up the coast by bus to Brownsville, Texas, Cobra then flew to Houston, from there
to Denver, Colorado, and from Denver to Lewiston,
Idaho. In Lewiston, using fake identification provided

her in Mexico, she rented a car at the Nez Perce County airport and drove east seventy-five miles through lightly falling snow to Trouth City. Cobra dialed Harmon White Bird from a pay phone at the Pony Up Cafe. A recording instructed her to leave a name and number and someone would call back soon. She had no choice but to give the pay phone number and wait.

Cobra took a seat at the counter. She was exhausted from her nonstop journey and did not notice that the three male customers in the place and the man behind the counter were all eyeballing her strangely. It did not occur to Cobra, preoccupied as she was by her mission, that an unescorted teenage African-American woman dressed in lightweight Mexican clothes would attract particular attention in a cafe in rural Idaho during mid-October. She noticed a calendar with a photo of a naked, blond-haired white woman on it tacked to the wall in front of her; all of the days of the month had been crossed out until the eighteenth. The heavyset, gray-red-bearded, middle-aged counterman moved into the space between Cobra and the calendar.

"What'll it be, miss?" he asked.

"It be my birthday," said Cobra.

The bearded man grinned. "Is that so? Name it, then, sister, and it's on the house."

Cobra pulled her cotton shawl closely around her shoulders and shivered. She recalled the taste of her mother Yarvella's okra gumbo on chilly January afternoons in New Orleans.

"Don't suppose you have any okra gumbo?" she said.

The burly man laughed. "No, ma'am. Not a specialty of the Pony Up and not likely to be. Got some hot leek and potato soup, though. That do?"

Cobra nodded. "Sounds wonderful."

The man brought her a large bowl of soup with three packages of saltine crackers on the side and a large spoon. Cobra took a sip.

"Y'all have any hot sauce?" she asked.

The man reached under the counter and came up with a bottle of Tabasco. Cobra peppered the soup with it and tried again.

"How's it now?" said the man.

"Almost perfect," said Cobra, giving him a big smile.

After she ate the soup and crackers, Cobra pushed

the bowl away, put her head down on the wooden counter, and fell sound asleep.

"Miss. Miss!"

Cobra felt a hand on her left arm, in which her head was cradled, and she sat up quickly. For a moment she had no idea where she was. Her vision was blurred and she shook her head to clear it.

"There's a telephone call for you," said the counterman, "if your name is Mary Jones."

"Yes, sir, it is. Thanks."

Cobra walked a bit unsteadily over to the phone and picked up the dangling receiver. She shuddered and saw that her Mexican shawl had fallen on the floor by the stool on which she had been sitting.

"Hello. This is Mary Jones."

"You wanted to speak to Harmon White Bird?"

"Yes."

"Harmon White Bird is dead."

"Dead?"

"Do yourself a favor, Mary Jones," said the voice on the other end of the line, which Cobra now recognized as female, "forget this telephone number."

"Wait, please! Do you know a man named DelRay Mudo?"

Cobra heard a click, followed by a dial tone. She hung up the phone. Cobra walked over and picked up her shawl. She saw that the cafe was empty except for herself and the bearded counterman. He approached her carrying a red three-quarter-length down coat. He draped the jacket over Cobra's shoulders.

"Happy birthday, miss," he said. "Welcome to the Great White North."

PASSPORT

FOLLOWING HER unsuccessful attempt to contact Harmon White Bird, Cobra decided to make a pilgrimage to Bad Leopard, Idaho, the birthplace of her late husband, Leander Ray Rhodes. As she drove Cobra debated with herself about what to do regarding the weapons purchase. The Countless Raindrops were depending on her to come through and she was puzzled by the disappearance of DelRay Mudo. These two things were foremost in her mind as she fought to negotiate the sleet-slippery mountain road.

Snow fascinated Cobra. It was a phenomenon all too rare in her experience. She remembered a time when she was five years old that snow fell on New

Orleans. This occurred late one February afternoon, paralyzing traffic throughout the city. The icy streets caused hundreds of accidents; motorists, discombobulated by the bizarre event, were forced to abandon their vehicles and trudge home through the ankle-deep, pristine precipitation.

Cobra and the other children at Reincarnation, however, were delighted. Wrapped up in their warmest clothes, the poorest progeny in N.O. reveled in the freak blizzard, building snowmen and having snowball fights for the first and what for many would be the only time in their lives. The dilapidated projects suddenly acquired a patina that transformed them into fairy-tale castles. Cobra wondered then and for years afterward how a conjureman or woman could have pulled off the "White Time" trick, as Courageous Jones, her then-nine-year-old cousin, also a resident of Reincarnation, called it.

Courageous Jones was murdered eight years later by an eleven-and-a-half-year-old girl named Cookie LaBête, whom he had impregnated. Cookie had demanded that Courageous come up with the money for an abortion but he refused to accept the responsibility. He told her he did not care what happened to her or the kid, that it was not his problem. Cookie took a .38 police special that her brother, Bagwell "Bag Man" LaBête, had stolen off a dead cop and hidden in his room, and shot Courageous Jones through his left earhole. As he lay bleeding to death on the ground in front of the Reincarnation laundry room a crowd gathered, and they bore witness as Cookie fired a second bullet point-blank into Courageous Jones's head, this time through his starboard aural orifice. "Now you got a problem ain' nobody can fix," she said, then spit at his twisted-up corpse.

Cobra switched on the radio.

"Known as the Lord's Resistance Army, the group has slain hundreds of villagers, often cutting off noses and ears, and kidnapped thousands of children. Operating out of the Gulu and Kitgum districts of Uganda, near the Sudanese border, the cult, formerly known as the Holy Spirit Movement, receives military aid from a Sudanese Islamic fundamentalist regime bent on destabilizing Uganda, which country's government they contend supports Christian rebels in the southern Sudan.

"The Lord's Army, a highly disciplined force equipped with assault weapons, machine guns, mortars and mines, adheres to a bizarre collection of 'commandments,' as they call them, including prohibitions against riding bicycles and eating the meat of white-feathered chickens. They murder adults indiscriminately but abduct children in order to indoctrinate them in their ways and to use as slave labor. The girls are raped and forced to bear children that can be raised as soldiers in the Lord's Army."

Cobra turned off the radio. "Damn!" she said. "Courageous Jones weren't nothin' compared to those people."

For a moment she considered the feasibility of contacting and purchasing arms from the Sudanese Muslims. Being African-American, Cobra figured, might work in her favor. Then again, Ugandans were people of color and their skin tone did nothing to mitigate against the unspeakable behavior practiced upon them by the Lord's Resistance Army. Race, Cobra Box decided, could be as undependable a passport as kindness.

PILGRIMAGE

IT WAS SNOWING hard on the road to Bad Leopard, so Cobra drove slowly. This kind of weather, as well as this part of the country, was new to her. She did not want to die on her pilgrimage. She remembered a story her late husband had told her about a boatload of men who were on a religious pilgrimage to a foreign land. One night in the middle of the ocean the ship, which was old and rusty, hit a reef and sprang a leak that could not be repaired. The captain, his officers and much of the crew escaped in lifeboats, abandoning the religious seekers who were traveling in steerage.

As the water crashed through the walls of the ship

the pilgrims fought their way to the deck from the hold in which they had been kept. As the freighter sank they watched the sailors row toward safety, certain that all was lost. The leader of the pilgrims led them in prayer while the men to whom they had entrusted their safe passage disappeared behind the crest of a wave.

As it happened, before the damaged freighter sank entirely, it was sighted by a passing ship and the holy men were rescued. Later the captain and officers of the death ship were brought to trial for dereliction of duty. The captain was publicly disgraced and officially rebuked, as were the other officers, all of whom were drummed out of the merchant service. Word of the captain's cowardice spread from port to port all over the world and he was forced to hire on as a wiper in the black gang of a coastwise trawler somewhere in the Far East.

After working in this menial capacity on inferior vessels in secret corners of the planet for several years, the former captain encountered the leader of the pilgrims whom he had abandoned. By this time the captain, haunted by that disaster, had destroyed himself with alcohol and careless behavior. Close to death, he begged the holy man for forgiveness. The man replied that it was the Lord's province and privilege to forgive, not His earthly servants'. He added, however, that the pilgrims' prayers as they were given up for lost on that fateful night had been for the captain and his crew. But why? asked the dying man. It is only through selflessness, answered the pilgrim, that the terrible becomes bearable. Too late for me, said the fallen captain. The pilgrim smiled and said, Therefore it is too late for us all.

A sign appeared on the side of the road:

BAD LEOPARD

POP. 108

MOOSE AND WOLVES

HAVE RIGHT-OF-WAY

Cobra drove on, enchanted by the sight of the snow-covered northern mountains. A half mile or so after the sign there was a gas station, but it appeared to be deserted. There was no sign of life anywhere.

The image of a Chinese Death Cage suddenly flashed into Cobra's mind. In one of Leander Ray's books of historical travel photographs she had seen a picture of a Chinese man in the nineteenth century who had been condemned to death for committing some serious crime. The method employed to carry out the sentence was a wooden platform fitted with a rope and constructed so that to avoid strangling himself the prisoner had to remain standing on his toes.

Cobra had no idea why she thought of this torture device now. When she had first seen the photo it horrified her. The condemned Chinese criminal's eyes appeared to be bursting to escape from his head as his toes wobbled and the dance of death was done. Curiously, the method of the Chinese Death Cage now seemed eminently sensible to Cobra. Nobody had to pull a trigger or switch, depress the plunger on a syringe, or cut a rope. Self-execution had more than a little to recommend it.

Cobra still had the image of the Chinese Death Cage in her mind when a wolf appeared in the road in front of her car. Just as suddenly, it disappeared. Cobra braked and stopped the vehicle. She sat there staring at the whiteness, wondering where to go. She turned on the radio. The Ink Spots were singing "I Don't Want to Set the World on Fire."

THE MOUTH OF TROUTH

COBRA DROVE BACK to Trouth City and checked into the Chief Joseph Hotel, which was, as far as she could tell, the only hotel in town. It was snowing hard and Cobra was exhausted and glad to get off the road. She couldn't wait to get into bed and sleep. The pilgrimage to Bad Leopard had been uneventful, and as there was no marker for where the Rhodes house once stood Cobra had not known where to stop to pay homage. When the storm picked up she headed back to Trouth City to reconsider her situation and get some rest.

As Cobra Box approached her room, number 36, on the second floor of the Chief Joseph Hotel, she saw a woman wearing a full-length beaver coat, a

Cleveland Indians baseball cap, and black, laced-up
Red Wing hiking boots standing in the hallway next
to the door of room 37. Cobra approached and
stopped in front of room 36, directly across from
where the woman stood.

"Hello," said Cobra.

The woman, whose age Cobra guessed was no
more than twenty-five, had bright red hair pulled back
into a ponytail, and violet eyes around which black
eyeliner had been smeared by tears. It was obvious to
Cobra that the woman was emotionally distraught.

"You all right?" Cobra asked.

The woman stood absolutely still for a moment,
then raised her right hand and showed Cobra a nickel-
plated hand cannon.

"Wayne walks out," she said, "he's a dead man."

Cobra inserted the key the desk clerk had given her
into the lock in the door of room 36 and opened it.

"Who's Wayne?"

"My husband. He's inside with my sister, Tanya. I
won't shoot her, she's blood. Wayne, though, he's a
dead duck."

"Do they know you're out here waitin' on 'em?"

The woman shook her head. "Don't think so.
Don't matter they do. Only way out is this door."

"Would you like to come in my room and sit down, maybe think this over?"

"No, thanks."

The woman took a good look at Cobra.

"You're black," she said.

Cobra smiled. "You noticed."

"Sorry—I mean, we don't see many black people up here in Idaho. It's a bit unusual, is all."

"My name is Cobra Box."

The woman offered her left hand. "Mine's Crystal Lake."

Cobra used her own left hand to squeeze Crystal's fingers.

"Sure you don't want to come in and talk?"

Cobra could not suppress a big yawn.

"You look pretty tired, Cobra Box. I'll be fine here. You go on and get your rest. Won't take but one bullet. Probably won't even wake you, you're sleepin' hard."

"You change your mind, just knock. Don't worry about wakin' me."

"Thanks, Cobra. Hey, where you from, anyway?"

"That's a good question, Crystal. New Orleans, I guess. I grew up there."

"Never been. Heard it's hot."

"Only snowed once in my memory."

"Sweet dreams, honey. You go on inside now."

Cobra closed the door behind her, threw off her coat and shoes, climbed into bed and immediately fell asleep. She dreamed that she was a little girl again, about eight years old, sitting on the front step of an apartment at Reincarnation with another girl. They were eating ice-cream cones, licking quickly before the heat melted them. The girls heard thunder, then looked up and saw a spiderleg of lightning reach out of the suddenly dark sky, creeping toward them. Cobra and the other little girl screamed and dropped their ice-cream cones as the electric limb hissed and crackled and scarred the concrete in front of where they sat. Black streaks were tattooed across the sidewalk, then they melted away, like the ice cream, and the dream was over.

When she woke up the next morning, the first thing Cobra did was look into the hallway. Crystal Lake was gone.

As Cobra ate breakfast at the Pony Up Cafe she read the *Mouth of Trouth*, the town newspaper. An article picked up from the Southern News Service caught her eye.

FEMALE KILLER COP CAPTURED
IN CRESCENT CITY SHOOT-OUT

NEW ORLEANS (SNS)—Contessa Sims, a two-year vet-
eran of the New Orleans police force, was captured
yesterday by fellow officers following a wild gun
battle in the Little Cambodia area of the city. Ofc.
Sims has been charged with extortion and murder
of six Cambodian immigrants, all members of the
Chan Doc family. The Chan Doc family owned the
Oriental Immortals restaurant on St. Bernard
Highway and evidently conducted an illegal gam-
bling operation at that location. Contessa Sims apparently knew of and abetted this enterprise. She
allegedly murdered the Chan Doc clan after they
refused to increase her share of the profits, attempting to disguise the killings as if they had occurred
during a robbery of the restaurant. Ofc. Sims was
apprehended at the Reincarnation housing project
on Orleans Street, where she lived as a child.

Cobra Box wept. Contessa Sims had been her closest friend when they were kids. Cobra realized that it
was Contessa with whom she had been sitting on the
step eating ice cream in her dream.

EVERYTHING DEPENDS ON THE WEATHER

COBRA RODE A series of trains to get from Idaho to Louisiana. As much as she desired to aid the Countless Raindrops, Cobra felt a stronger pull at her heart from Contessa Sims, so she took off for New Orleans. The morning she arrived Cobra went immediately to see her mother, Yarvella, who had moved out of Reincarnation into a small house on Elba near the corner of South Dupre. Cobra's surprise appearance at her door both thrilled and shocked her mother.

"Cobra! My baby!" Yarvella shrieked when she saw her daughter standing on the doorstep.

She opened the door and grabbed Cobra, squeezing her tightly.

"You almos' gave your mama a heart attack! Why didn't you tell me you were comin'?"

Cobra embraced Yarvella and let the tears come.

"Mama, I'm just so happy to be here. I'll tell you everything soon, I promise. So much happen since I left New Orleans."

"Okay, darlin'. I'm just so glad to have you back!"

"Mama, you got my last letter?"

"You mean about Leander Ray bein' killed?"

Cobra nodded.

"I'm so sorry about that, child. Times must been hard for you in Mexico. You here to stay, I hope."

"I'm not sure, Mama. I'm here for a while, anyway. I read about Contessa bein' arrested."

"Ain't that terrible? Say she kill six people."

"Is it true, Mama? What do you think?"

"I don't know. Misterioso and Lola Mae claim their daughter was set up. Hard to tell. People say she got up with a Asian dope ring."

"Maybe I can help her."

"I pray for Contessa. She always been a sweet child."

Cobra took a nap in a back bedroom Yarvella said she had kept fixed for her daughter's eventual return. Cobra's brother, Fidel, Yarvella told her, was doing fine in the Marine Corps. Leander Ray had set Fidel on the right road, and for that, as well as his pension payments, Yarvella would always be grateful to him.

That evening Cobra went to see Misterioso and Lola Mae Sims. Misterioso, Contessa's father, was a dour man whose bitterness nobody dared challenge. He had lost both of his legs from just above the knees when the car he was driving collided head-on with a city bus. The bus driver, who suffered from chronic depression, had fallen asleep after taking too many nerve pills and allowed his bus to drift into the path of oncoming traffic. Misterioso was thirty-one years old at the time. The bus driver, a forty-nine-year-old resident of the ninth ward named Pedro "Pork Chop" Parker, was decapitated during the accident when the careening bus ricocheted off Misterioso Sims's crunched car into a streetlight standard that penetrated the front window and sheared off Pork Chop's top.

Since this unfortunate occurrence Misterioso spent most of his time sitting in a wheelchair in front of building D at Reincarnation with a loaded .32-caliber Smith & Wesson single- and double-action revolver in his lap, hoping some crackhead would attempt to mug him. "It'll be me or him," Sims threatened, "and I don't give a rooster's red-speckled ass which!" Even though he had received a sizeable cash settlement plus lifetime disability payments from the city, Misterioso refused to move out of the project. When Lola Mae suggested they do so, Sims responded, "Anywhere but here, a man without no legs be a freak."

When Cobra Box arrived at the Sims residence, Misterioso was asleep in his wheelchair in front of the television in the living room, his gun in his lap. The television set was on but the volume was turned all the way down. From where Cobra sat on the sofa talking to Lola Mae she could see half-naked white girls who seemed to have trouble keeping their hair out of their eyes running around on a beach.

"It ain't possible Contessa did what they say," said Lola Mae. "She worked hard to get on the force. No way she ruin her dream. Contessa ain't no killer."

"I want to help," said Cobra. "Does Contessa have a good attorney?"

"Man named R. P. Dufour. R. P. stand for Robes and Pierre. Ads on TV say, 'Let me DO-FOR you.' I suppose he's doin' best he can. Papers say it's an open and shut case, seein' how there's witnesses to the murders."

"Who are they?"

"Teenage brother and sister that was hidin' when

the shootin' go down. Don't know how they could see who did it, they was hid so good."

"Guess I'll go see this Dufour. What's Contessa say?"

"Say she show up as regular her moonlight security job, find everybody dead. Phone line was cut, so she go find a pay phone. Nex' thing she know cops unloadin' on her. Somehow she get away, try an' come home to me and Misterioso. Police arrest Contessa outside our door 'bout four in the mornin'. Girl didn't even have her gun."

"Where was it?"

"Police say they find it in a trash bin by the Immoral Oriental restaurant. Got to be it was planted. Contessa don't do this, Cobra. You know the girl."

Lola Mae, a heavyset, orange-colored woman with straight purple-black hair, began to sob. Cobra held her. Misterioso woke up and saw his wife weeping on Cobra Box's chest. He used a remote control to turn up the sound on the television.

"Drop him, Patsy," said a blond girl wearing a flimsy red halter top to a brunette in a skin-tight black wetsuit. "You knew Rob's reputation when you started going out with him. He's always been a bad-weather day at the beach."

The brunette, Patsy, tossed her head to get the hair out of her eyes. She stared out at the water for a moment, watched a wave curl and crash and die on the sand before looking again at the other girl.

"Paula," she said, "I...I think I'm pregnant."

ABOGADO

"Miz Box, what I can do *you* for?"

Robespierre "R. P." Dufour, a tall, skeletal man, seated himself behind a desk across from his interlocutor. Cobra's first thought upon seeing Contessa's lawyer was that he looked like James Stewart, if the actor were ravaged and withered by AIDS.

"I come to inquire about the case of Contessa Sims, Mr. Dufour."

"R. P., please. Precisely what is your relationship to Officer Sims?"

"She about my oldest friend in the world."

"I see."

Dufour removed a long green cigar from a wooden box on the desk.

"Mind if I smoke, Cobra?"

"No, sir."

"Mind that I call you by your Christian name?"

"No."

Dufour struck a match and puffed on the cigar until it glowed.

"Don't rightly know if Cobra be Christian, exactly. I do like the *resonance* of it, though, you know what I mean."

"I hear there witnesses say Contessa the shooter."

"What the DA claim."

"Mr. Dufour...."

"R. P."

"Contessa couldn't do this. My mama tell me two of the victims children, ages six an' eight. No way the Contessa Sims I know would do such a thing."

Dufour worked his cigar as he spoke. "How long has it been since you've seen Officer Sims?"

"Two, maybe two and one-half years. I been away."

"Things happen can change a person in a lot less'n that amount of time. But I agree with you, Cobra. I don't think she committed these murders. I do believe she's covering up for someone, however. I'll lay ten to one Contessa knows the guilty party. My guess is she was partnered in a shakedown, protectin' the illegal gamblin' setup. Could be the Chan Doc clan resisted a request to increase the payout."

"Maybe Contessa's afraid to talk."

Dufour puffed hard and contemplated the smoke cloud.

"Think she'll talk to you about it?"

"I don't know. I'd like to see her, though."

"I'll fix it. Leave your telephone number with my secretary."

Cobra stood up. "Thanks, Mr. Dufour. You been kind." She extended her right hand.

Dufour remained seated but took Cobra's hand in his own and held it tightly. She could feel the bones through his paper-thin skin. The air between them was hazy green.

"I'm capable of even greater acts of kindness, Cobra. We'll meet again."

Cobra extracted her hand. As she flexed her fingers her brain conjured up the indelible image of Ava Varazo firing on Thankful Priest.

COBRA GETS IT RIGHT

COBRA BOX SAT on the visitor's side of the thick plastic window waiting for Contessa Sims to be brought in. Cobra had been in the Orleans Parish jail before— twice, in fact—to visit her brother, Fidel: once after he had been arrested for assault (charge dropped before case got to trial), another time for attempted robbery (insufficient evidence, case dismissed). She hated this place; it stank of rot despite the heavy use of Lysol that made her nostrils feel as if they had been invaded by stinging gnats. The acrid disinfectant did nothing to dispel the olfactory-induced image of a stagnant pool choked by dozens of poisoned fish floating belly-up on the surface. Cobra closed her eyes and watched a big bull gator, unperturbed by the stench, stretch open its gruesome maw and chomp down on a bunch of inert bluegills.

A steel door clanked and Cobra opened her eyes. Seconds later Contessa sat on the other side of the window staring at her. Both women picked up the phones placed on the ledges in front of them.

"Hey, Tess. How you doin'?"

"Holdin' up, Cob. 'Bout you? How was Mexico?"

"That's a long story. Short and sad part is Leander Ray got killed."

"Oh, girl, I'm sorry. You come back home, huh?"

"For now. Stayin' with Mama."

"How she's doin'?"

"Fine. New house looks good. She happy there."

"Good she got out the homes. It get worse there all the time."

"Tess, what I can do for you?"

Contessa laughed. "Sound like you been talkin' to a certain lawyer."

"R. P. fix it so I can come see you."

"R. P., huh? Don't trust the man, Cobra. Don't trust any man." Contessa bit her lower lip. "You want to know I did this thing."

"I already know. Know before I come here. Contessa Sims ain't no killer."

"I love you, girl, you know that."

"Love you, too."

"All right, then."

A guard appeared behind Contessa. Cobra looked up at him. She saw his thin lips move but could not hear what he said. Contessa placed the palm of her left hand flat against the window. Cobra matched it.

"Thought we had fifteen minutes."

"They change the rules suit theyselves."

"How I can help, Tess?"

"R. P. be in touch. Thanks for comin', Cob. Hug Yarvella for me."

Cobra stood outside at Tulane and Broad. A small breeze froze the beads of sweat on her forehead, causing her to shiver. The afternoon sky was clouding up quickly. All of the people passing by looked ugly, uglier than usual. Cobra suddenly doubled over and vomited on the sidewalk. When she had finished, Cobra wiped her mouth with the flat of her right hand.

"Can I do something for you?"

Cobra looked up and saw a middle-aged white

man dressed in a tan suit. He wore silver wire-rimmed eyeglasses, was clean shaven and mostly bald. A purple birthmark the size of a Barq's bottlecap decorated his left cheek.

"Mister," she said, "nothin' you could do for anybody would ever be enough."

CORREO AÉREO

Dear Ava and Everyone Fight the Good Fight
I am report in from New Orleans not Idaho where I
was unable to find Harmon White Bird or learn what
happen to DelRay Mudo. I know you dependin on
me to deal for the weapons but when I was in the
North I find out my oldest best friend be in serus
trouble down home so I come. I want you please
understand my heart be with you all right now tho
I feel my place be here. This a small fry compare to
your people struggle but my friend Contessa she
need me. I be in touch soon I promise.

Your Sister
Cobra Box

HOW HEAVEN SLIPPED UP

COBRA WAS NOT entirely displeased to be back in New Orleans, living with her mother. The world and its troubles had risen about to Cobra's ears and she was doing all she could to keep from drowning in the sea of misery. Aside from Contessa Sims, another of Cobra's old friends from Reincarnation had slipped up, a girl named Heaven Cure.

Heaven Cure had always been a small-sized person, the littlest child among her age group at the project. Fully grown she stood only four foot ten and a half inches, but Heaven had a beautiful figure, green cat's eyes, and a naturally sweet expression on her mango-colored face. Men were wild for her and she had her pick of the locals. When she chose to marry Hernando "Big Cut" Crockett, it caused no small amount of distress to her mother, Ruby Ponds Cure, whose husband, Heaven's father, Ebony George, had died of a heart attack when Heaven was thirteen. Hernando Crockett was called Big Cut because of his habit since childhood of always taking the largest portion of pie, cake, or steak, whatever was on the table. Big Cut was a huge man, six foot seven, his weight in the vicinity of 340 pounds. It was not his size, however, that troubled Ruby Ponds Cure, but his profession. Crockett controlled crack cocaine traffic at the Reincarnation, Iberville, Florida, and Desire housing projects. That this monster could have charmed her most precious only child into marrying him devastated Ruby Cure.

Yarvella Box and Ruby's other good friends did their best to comfort her, but Ruby was beside herself with sorrow. Heaven's attitude did nothing to dispel her mother's mood, telling Ruby only that Hernando was the kindest, gentlest man she had ever known, that he treated her respectfully and thrilled her the way no other man had. The fact that he was a drug dealer did not disquiet Heaven.

"He don't rip nobody off," she told her mother. "Hernando a fair man in everything he do."

Marrying Big Cut Crockett was one thing, but how Heaven Cure came to slip up most seriously resulted from her having a man on the side. This was a situation not even Heaven's closest friends suspected. That it was a white man with whom Heaven was involved did not particularly surprise anybody, but when it was revealed that he was one of New Orleans's most prominent citizens, Durance Vieil, president of the Cabildo Bank, tongues gagged and wagged.

Cobra heard the story from O'Kay Fannie Taylor, a former Reincarnation resident who now lived down the street from Yarvella. According to O'Kay, Heaven had met the man at his bank, where she regularly visited Big Cut Crockett's safety deposit boxes. Mr. Vieil struck up a conversation with her one day, and thereafter, following Heaven's deposit or withdrawal, she and Durance would lunch and afterward repair to a suite he kept at the Hotel Jetta on Magazine Street.

Why Heaven would become involved with Vieil was a question nobody would ever answer, seeing as how Hernando Crockett made his biggest cuts of all across the throats of the trysting pair before an explanation could be offered.

"Big Cut didn't never really trust nobody," O'Kay

Fannie told Cobra Box. "He had Heaven followed sometime without her knowin'. When his man Donnell Spells report back 'bout Heaven goin' in a side entrance the Jetta with this dude, he was confuse'. Donnell say Big Cut make out like he know all about it, that Heaven was settin' Vieil up for some game. But Donnell say Big Cut don't sound convince'. Nex' time Heaven go to the safety deposit Big Cut tell Donnell, follow her again. When he come back with the same story, Big Cut don't say nothin'.

"Few days later it's on the TV news. Vieil an' Heaven practic'ly decapitated in the hotel room, blood everywhichwhere—bed, walls, rugs—an' Big Cut shot to death in the lobby, where the security mens chase him. Picture of Big Cut laid out flat with a butcher knife in his hand bleedin' into the marble floor on the front page nex' mornin's *Times-Picayune*.

"What you suppose Heaven be up to with that outside man, Cobra? I mean, she *dug* Hernando."

"Hard to say, O'Kay. Saw a old movie on TV where a gypsy woman says at the end, 'What do it matter what you say about a person?' It don't work tryin' to figure this kinda shit out."

CHILDREN OF PARADISE

DONNELL SPELLS was fifteen and Cobra Box eleven when he kidnapped her. Cobra was walking home from school alone at the time. She was two blocks from Reincarnation and Donnell crept up behind her, picked up the girl, and carried her off. Spells had stolen a car and drove Cobra and himself to an empty lot next to the railroad tracks at Ferdinand Street and Florida Avenue, where he attempted to rape her in the front seat.

Cobra grabbed Donnell's testicles in her right hand and squeezed them as hard as she could. Spells screamed and released his hold on her. Cobra bolted from the car. At that moment a Norfolk Southern freight train barreled by, forcing Cobra to run alongside the line of boxcars. She did not look around to see if Donnell Spells was following her but she tripped and fell, anyway. Cobra saw that she had stumbled over the body of a white woman. She looked back from where she lay on the ground toward the car and saw that it was gone.

Cobra studied the body. The woman was not moving and her blue eyes were wide open. She was about twenty to thirty years old and wore a white T-shirt with the words BACK OFF BITCH on the front, blue satin shorts and a pink bandanna tied around her head. Her scraggly black hair was chopped short. She was taller than Cobra, about five foot one, but she weighed much more. The woman's mouth was open and Cobra could see two gold front teeth. On her left leg, behind the knee, was tattooed the letter V; on her right leg, also behind the knee, was tattooed the number 6. Bugs were crawling in and out of the woman's ears, mouth and nostrils.

The train had passed by before Cobra got to her feet. She crossed the tracks and ran all the way home. Cobra never told anyone about being kidnapped or finding the body. Donnell Spells disappeared from around Reincarnation and Cobra hoped that he was as dead as that bad-haired white woman.

FLYING DOWN TO CAIRO

COBRA BOX WALKED along the boardwalk next to the Mississippi River. It was ten P.M. but the sky still retained a measure of tropical pink. A half-moon lit the gently rippling water: a celestial torch, its whiteness flickering as slender clouds slid across the flame, manipulating the shadows like *Bunraku*. Two tugboats, the *Hard Way* and the *Merry Me*, shoved a black barge toward Algiers. Cobra was thinking about the strange turns her life had taken in the past two years: her marriage to Leander Ray Rhodes, life with the rebels in Mexico, Lee's death, the aborted trip to Idaho, Contessa's case acting as a signal for her to return to New Orleans. Cobra thought about Ava Varazo, the most strong-minded woman she had ever met. It was Cobra's desire to be like Ava, only she was unsure as to her real direction in life. Right now, Cobra decided, she would take it one step at a time.

She tripped and very nearly fell. A hand caught Cobra by the left shoulder and helped her regain her balance.

"Careful, lady."

Cobra stood up straight again and saw a brown boy no more than thirteen years old grinning at her.

"Thanks. I must have caught my heel in between the planks."

"Good thing Cairo Fly was passin' by."

"Who?"

"Cairo Fly. That's my name."

"Kay what?"

"C-a-i-r-o. Pronounced Kay-ro, like Cairo, Illinois, city upriver where I was born. My mama and I moved to New Orleans when I was three, almost ten years ago."

Cobra looked him over. He was about five foot three, too skinny, but the boy had Tony Curtis hair and extraordinarily beautiful emerald green eyes that glowed under the soft evening light. He was wearing a dirty white T-shirt, khaki shorts, and torn-up sneakers without socks.

"You live with your mama, Cairo?"

"No, she's gone. What's your name?"

"Cobra Box."

The boy laughed. "Your name's funny as mine."

Cobra smiled. "Can't argue that."

"You live with your mama?"

Cobra hesitated, then said, "I guess I do. Who do you live with?"

"Nobody. I'm on my own now."

"How long ago did your mama die?"

"Didn't die, she left."

"Where to?"

Cairo Fly shrugged and looked out at the river.

"Are you hungry, Cairo? Do you want to come home with me and get some supper?"

The boy turned his face back to Cobra and smiled. He had large grayish yellow teeth.

"Your mama won't mind?"

"Come on. Take forty minutes to walk there."

"You ain't got no car?"

Cobra had already started walking. Cairo Fly followed and fell into step next to her.

"Do you go to school?"

"Not lately."

"You have any other family here?"

"Uh-uh. It was always just me and Mama."

"Where do you sleep, Cairo?"

"I got places nobody bother me."

A light rain began to fall. Cairo repeatedly ran his hands through his long, curly hair, rinsing it as he walked.

"What's your mama's name?"

"Carol. She's white."

"And you really don't have any idea where she be?"

"Maybe Illinois. I'll be flyin' down to Cairo sometime myself, find my daddy, you know? Soon as I got the fare."

At the northeast corner of Melpomene and Magnolia a man was lying face down on the sidewalk. His dark brown short-brim hat had fallen into the gutter. Cairo kicked the body but got no response. The boy quickly went through the man's pockets and found a few coins, which he placed in one of his own pockets.

Cobra shouted, "*¡Zopilote!*"

"What?"

"A *zopilote* is a Mexican vulture, a bird that preys on the dead."

"Man ain't dead, just drunk."

Cairo picked up the hat and tried it on.

"You ever see a vulture wear a brim?"

Cobra walked on. The rain was falling harder. Cairo kept the hat, even though it sat on his ears, and hurried after her.

When Yarvella saw Cairo's eyes she gasped and crossed herself. "Cobra!" she cried. "Who you bring into my house?"

"A homeless boy, Mama. He's hungry. Name be Cairo Fly."

" 'They wandered in the wilderness in a solitary way,' " said Yarvella; " 'they found no city to dwell in. Hungry and thirsty, their soul fainted in them.' "

" 'Oh that men would praise the Lord for his goodness, and for his wonderful works to the children of men!' " Cobra recited. " 'For he satisfieth the longing soul, and filleth the hungry soul with goodness.' I remember my Bible, too, Mama."

Cairo Fly removed the hat and displayed his gray-yellow teeth to Yarvella.

"Pleased to meet you, Miz Box."

Cobra was surprised to see that even indoors Cairo's eyes glowed.

CHRISTMAS IN NEW ORLEANS

THE NEXT MORNING both Yarvella and Cobra were awakened by the sound of a piano being played. They got up and went into the front room and saw Cairo Fly sitting at Yarvella's old upright, his fingers on the keys. The piano had been a gift to Yarvella from her church, the Serpent in the Wilderness Sanctified, in whose gospel group, the Serpent's Tongues, she had sung for thirty years. The night before, after feeding him, Cobra had handed Cairo a pillow and a blanket and told him that he was welcome to sleep on the couch, which offer he gratefully accepted.

When he saw that the women were in the room, the boy began to sing:

I was in New Orleans last Christmas
So low down I had to cry
I was in New Orleans on Christmas
So low down I had to cry
I was sittin' on the sidewalk
Everybody pass me by

It's sad to be alone at Christmas
In New Orleans or anywhere
It's so sad to be alone at Christmas
In New Orleans or anywhere
When you're broke down and hungry
And you don't got no one to care

I was sittin' on the sidewalk
Thinkin' how to ease my pain
I was sittin' on the sidewalk
Thinkin' on how to ease my pain
If I had a loaded pistol
Might put a bullet in my brain

Felt a touch upon my shoulder
A voice said Brother, come with me
Felt a hand upon my shoulder
Voice said rise and walk with me
I looked up and saw an angel
The kindest face I'll ever see

———

Won't be alone again at Christmas
In New Orleans or anywhere
I'll never be alone at Christmas
Not in N.O. or anywhere
In the company of angels
I found the answer to my prayer.

Cairo Fly turned toward the Box women and smiled. It was then that they noticed he was wearing Yarvella's pair of faux teardrop diamond earrings, ruby red lipstick, rouge and eyeliner.

"Boy," said Cobra, "you full of surprises."

BIBLE STORY

YARVELLA GAVE the Fly boy twenty dollars, a new compact of Maybelline blush and told him to keep the tube of ruby red lipstick he had already used. Cobra embraced Cairo and told him to keep in touch, that she and her mother were there for him.

"You ladies take good care, now," he said.

" 'Remember how short my time is,' " said Yarvella. " 'Wherefore hast thou made all men in vain?' Keep the Lord in mind, Cairo, 'For he shall give his angels charge over thee, to keep thee in all thy ways.' "

"I keep that thought, Miz Box. Thanks."

After Cairo Fly had gone, Yarvella said, "Cobra, baby, the world ain't heard the last of that boy."

"Mama, the world ain't even heard the first. I just hope his heart be strong as his attitude."

Six months later a letter arrived postmarked Chicago, Illinois. In it was a twenty-dollar bill, a note and a newspaper article.

Dear Box Ladys. I work in a man club call Chicken in A Basket. The mony real good. I cut this out it a Bible story. Love C.Fly

6 EGYPTIANS DIE TRYING TO
SAVE DROWNING CHICKEN

CAIRO—Six people drowned yesterday while trying to rescue a chicken that had fallen into a well.

An 18-year-old farmer was the first to descend into the 60-foot well. He drowned, apparently after an undercurrent in the water pulled him down, police said.

His sister and two brothers, none of whom could swim well, went in one by one to help him, but also drowned. Two elderly farmers then came to help, but they apparently were pulled down by the same undercurrent.

The bodies of the six were later pulled out of the well in the village of Nazlat Imara, 240 miles south of Cairo.

The chicken was also pulled out. It survived.

NAKED

IN THE EARLY MORNING of the day on which Contessa
Sims's case was to go to trial she was found hanging
nude in her cell. A guard cut her down immediately
but the medical examiner determined that she had
been dead for approximately thirty minutes before he
did so. Officer Sims used her jail clothing, which she
had torn into strips and tied together, to accomplish
the task.

When Cobra Box heard the news on the radio she
was dressing to go to the courthouse to attend the
trial. She shivered and lay down on her bed, her body
numb. Cobra recalled a story her late husband,
Leander Ray, had told her concerning a man he had

read about in the *Journal of Forensic Sciences* who hanged himself suspended by a rope attached to the raised shovel of a diesel-powered backhoe. The man, a beet farmer in California, was discovered in a partially seated position with a cloth safety harness strap wrapped around his neck and clipped to the rope. The farmer had used the ligature to achieve partial autoerotic asphyxiation, then lost consciousness and accidentally hanged.

Contessa Sims had always been a strong-minded person, thought Cobra, but as it was written in the Book of Judges, Contessa's soul was vexed unto death. At least that lonely beet farmer had gotten a final kick out of it.

COBRA BOX RECEIVED in the mail from Mexico a small, stained, battered, and torn purple-covered notebook. On the first inside page, hand printed in large letters, were the words *El Cuaderno Amoratado* ("The Black-and-Blue—or 'Bruised'—Notebook"). It was a trick diary kept by Ava Varazo in Sinaloa, Texas. Only a few of the pages had writing on them, all of it in Spanish.

PART FOUR

El Cuaderno amoratado

la polla cubierta de verrugas quiere que
le chupe los huevos pero no se pone
tiesa hace que le pise la cara primero
con un pie luego con el otro

cock covered with warts wanted me to suck

his balls couldnt get hard made me stand

on his face one foot at a time

un tío muy gordo y muy borracho me
pide que me ponga un vestido blanco y
le cante la Golondrina se mea en los
calzoncillos tengo que limpiar el suelo

very fat man very drunk asked me to put on

white dress and sing La Golondrina he

pissed his pants had to clean the floor

miope de un ojo una polla enorme
doblada hacia abajo se está mucho rato
hace ver que no se corre me lo saco de
encima y le digo que ha de pagar más él
me llama hija de la gran puta

short one eye big cock bent down took a long

time tried to pretend he didnt come pushed

him off told him he had to pay more called

me murdering whore mother

hace que me siente de espaldas encima
de su cara y se la frote con el culo la
polla no se le mueve me dice que no se
la toque

made me sit on his face backwards rub my ass

over it his cock didnt move told me not to

touch it

mamada a un viejo se le pone dura pero
no se corre me da un beso en la
coronilla y me llama Rosita o Rosalita
dice que es el nombre de su hija

old man sucked he got hard but couldnt come

kissed me on top of my head called me Rosita

or Rosalita his daughters name he said

gringo jovan quiere plantarme un cruci-
fijo EN El coño y hacerme una foto lE
digo que SE busque otra

young gringo wanted to stick crucifix in my cunt

take a picture told him get a different girl

dos hombres uno mira mientras el otro
folla el que mira suda más que el que
me folla

two men one watched while the other fucked

man who watched sweated more than the one

who fucked me

las dos orejas cortadas cara manos y
brazos llenos de cicatrices no habla
pero folla como un bestia huele a lima

both ears cut off face hands and arms full of

scars didnt talk fucked hard smelled of lime

guapo pero con una polla enana se me
sienta encima del pecho se la casco
hasta que se corre en mi cara y luego
me la limpia a lametazos

handsome but smallest cock ever sat on my

chest jacked him off until he came on my

face then he licked it clean

me limpia el coño y el culo luego me
estruja las tetas y me da las gracias

washed my cunt and asshole then squeezed

my breasts said thank you

uN Poli sE quita El uNiforme ya la tiENE
dura PEro sE corrE aNtEs dE metérmela
y luEgo ya No hay maNera dE quE sE lE
PoNga tiEsa

cop took off his uniform his cock was

already hard but came before he could

put it in and couldnt get hard again

tipo limpio y callado me folla se
levanta y luego cae muerto con los
calcetines puestos

clean quiet man fucked got up fell down

dead with red socks on

dos tipos feos me follan como locos
por el culo uno me pega varias veces y
luego se mea en mi cara iban armados

two ugly men both fucked me hard in the

ass one hit me a few times then pissed

on my face they had guns

bailo una vez no más de aída Cuevas a
la luz de una vela con sólo unas bragas
negras el tio se echa a llorar

danced to Una Vez No Más by Aída Cuevas

wearing only a black slip in candle light he

cried

BALL OF FIRE

COBRA BOX BOUGHT a box of saltine crackers and a pink lemonade Snapple in Elgrably's Grocery on the corner of Salcedo and Clio. She came out of the store and turned right toward South Gayoso, unscrewing the bottle top as she walked. It was a cloudy, humid morning, just past eleven. Cobra stopped, lifted the lemonade to her lips and drank. Suddenly she was hit on the left side of her face, a blow that sent the box of crackers and the bottle flying. Cobra heard glass shatter on the sidewalk and the next thing she knew she was being dragged into the street. A large, heavily muscled arm was wrapped tightly around Cobra's chest. She was woozy from being punched and did not resist as her assailant stuffed her into a car and pushed the young woman down onto the floor beneath the dashboard. A door slammed and Cobra heard footsteps, then another door slammed and the car began to move. She opened her eyes but the vision was blurred.

"Don't talk! Don't move!"

Cobra's eyes focused. She stared directly into the barrel of a gun. It was being gripped by a stocky dark brown man. The man's head was pear shaped, mostly bald; and he had a thick black mustache. He was wearing a gray sweat-stained T-shirt and dirty lime green slacks. The car smelled bad, like the urine of a person who has recently eaten asparagus.

Cobra felt the car jerk, stop, go again. It passed under a viaduct and up a ramp. She knew he was heading for the highway. Cobra went for the gun, striking at it with both hands, knocking the man's arm sideways. The gun fell from his hand and disappeared into the well between the seat and the passenger door. The man took his right foot off of the accelerator pedal and kicked Cobra twice, once on the mouth, the second time, as she turned away, above her right ear. Cobra reached for the passenger door handle, yanked down hard and dived out of the car. She hit the ground head first and immediately lost consciousness, which is why she did not feel the car's right rear tire roll over her left foot.

Four days later, when Cobra woke up, the first thing she noticed was her elevated left leg, the foot of which was encased in a metal boot attached to several wires strung from the ceiling. The second thing she noticed was that she could not see out of her right eye; it was patched with a rubber-edged disk and sealed by a bandage. She did not hear a sound.

Cobra closed her left eye. She saw the early-morning sky over La Villanía. It was pale blue and entirely devoid of clouds. A red-tailed hawk came into view, gliding on a zephyr. Cobra watched the hawk drift until it suddenly swooped down and snatched her up. She was surprised at how gently the hawk clasped her in its talons, and Cobra relaxed as the bird gained altitude. From aloft she saw an angel standing in the sun, beckoning. It was toward the ball of fire that the hawk bore Cobra Box.

PART FIVE

CODA

DIMINUENDO

MAN APPARENTLY LEFT
FOR DEAD SURVIVES

LOS ANGELES—A 30-year-old man who survived a botched execution-style attempt on his life Friday night was found bleeding but alive in a ditch next to Mulholland Drive in the Hollywood Hills.

Los Angeles County Sheriff's sergeant Sueña Sabandija said the unidentified man was found shortly after two A.M. by motorists.

Sabandija said the man had been shot several times and toppled over an embankment, but he managed to crawl back up close to the road, collapsing in a muddy spot.

Officers are looking for two women and four men involved in the shooting, according to authorities.

The victim has a tattoo on his left forearm of two snakes entwined in the shape of a heart around the words "DelRay Loves Ava."

THE FOUR MEN, who called themselves White Horse, Geronimo, Natches and Fun, after the last Apache warriors; and the two women, whose names came from the Song of Solomon, Rose of Sharon and Lily of the Valleys, were encamped in the Old Woman Mountains, east of Cadiz. They had come to this place to await the occasion, which they were certain was imminent, when the sun would stand still in the midst of heaven for an entire day. They believed this phenomenon would be a signal that the New Canaanites had been expunged from the face of the planet by the Lord's own hand; that it was safe for His earthly angels, who had taken refuge in the wilderness following the Crimson Crusade, to return to the cities.

The four men and two women lay together under the stars.

"Only those who have taken heed of His Word will survive this holocaust, called the Final Truth in the Unwritten Knowings," said Fun, the bravest of the band.

Rose of Sharon, who, unbeknownst to her, was carrying Geronimo's child, gave witness: "And out of His mouth goeth a sharp sword."

CON MUCHO CARIÑO

THE FOLLOWING LETTER, without an envelope, was discovered in one of DelRay's pockets by the police. After he regained consciousness he was found to be suffering from total amnesia, probably as a result of severe trauma. The attending physician, in an attempt to jog DelRay's memory, showed him the letter, but DelRay had no recollection of the author.

Dear DelRay,

I am sitting on my bed writing this letter. Lights off. I have lit five candles to the Virgin Mary. What's your wish? My grandmother was a firm believer in the Rosary. Every time we got in the car if we were going more than ten miles she would pull out the beads. When my father went into the army she went to the statue of Saint Jude to say prayers. Two weeks later he broke his leg so badly that he was given a medical discharge and didn't have to go to the war. Days before her husband, my grandfather, died he claimed to have seen an angel. He would sit in his bed and talk about this angel and how beautiful she was. Sometimes I think it was my grandmother that he saw because in my mind she was better than any angel. My grandfather told me the story of the singer Yolanda del Rio—La Hija de Nadie—when she was a baby her father took her brother, who was five years old at the time, and left. Years later, Yolanda's twin sister met a man and they fell in love. It turned out that he was her long lost brother. The two were so devastated when they found out they committed suicide together. Their father disappeared again and their mother died of sadness shortly thereafter. No wonder Yolanda del Rio always sounds like she's crying when she sings!

Actually here's the whole story as it was in the movie of Yolanda's life. Yolanda's mother has twin girls, Yolanda and Ines. The father leaves, taking his older son. The father is a big-time drunk. The girls grow up being made fun of all the time by other kids cause they don't have a father. Yolanda's mother and sister fall down a flight of stairs after putting out a fire. The mother dies and the sister goes blind. One day the sister is walking and bumps into a man, they knock heads and she regains her sight! Of course they fall in love. But they find out they are brother and sister so they commit suicide. Then Yolanda gets in a car wreck and loses her memory for a while. After she recovers it she goes searching for the only other living members of her family—her father and brother. She ends up in a gypsy camp with a bunch of midgets. Her father shows up but can't face her, he's too ashamed. I don't know what happened to the brother but shortly after Yolanda finds out this man is her father the gypsy queen tosses a knife at him, hits him in the heart—EL FIN. Well my friend that's somethin' else. ¿Que no? And it's supposed to be true.

There's a strange man who lives two doors down in this rooming house. He always wears sunglasses and a bandanna and I've seen him a few times leaving his room at night with a lantern to light his way. Usually he has a Band-Aid someplace on his face. Above his door he has a little concave mirror so he can see down the hallway. I made an interesting discovery yesterday. Outside his door I picked up from the floor a piece of piano wire with a key ring welded on each side. I figure the guy dropped it. I'm keeping it as a souvenir. I'm not too worried, even though he's probably paranoid and psychopathic. From what I hear those types prey on the vulnerable, so I guess that makes it a good thing that I only look vulnerable on paper.

The world is getting crazier day by day and people have been pissing me off left and right. My guardian demons have been working overtime. Did I tell you about them? Some people have guardian angels. I have guardian demons who go to work when people piss me off. The other day my boss made me angry and I thought of all the bad things I could wish on him which would not be so bad as to cause bodily harm but sufficient enough to cause him some inconvenience and better yet loss of face. I decided that it would be good if he crashed his new car. Two days later this occurred. No injuries to either party and the "accident" was his fault. I also threw an evil eye at one of my coworkers who has since hurt his back. His dog also died after I told him it was stupid and was going to grow up to be one of those dogs that pees on you when it gets excited. This is almost too much to handle. Like when my Uncle Lodo evicted a poor family from a house he owned. Before he went through with it the people told him that if he did everything would go bad for him. He laughed about this in my presence and said they threatened to call the witch doctor on him. I gave him a scary look and said Some people don't need witch doctors. The next day the IRS seized all of his properties and belongings. They'd discovered he'd been collecting disability payments for decades for a dead person. He's gonna be singing Johnny Cash songs soon.

My father always warns his girlfriends not to mess with me because I "do things". He says I have a special light around me and those who are close to me are protected by it. I don't know about that. A boyfriend of mine once started a bunch of shit with me and he got three traffic tickets in less than 24 hours. It's kind of scary and I have sought professional help on two occasions. Once the priest who was about a million years old told me I was "a great temptation" to him, then put his hand on my thigh. On another occasion a priest said to me We don't believe in that sort of thing any more. So I guess I'll just have to live with it.

I had a bad cold last week. I stayed home on Saturday night in front of the tv watching Acapulco Caliente. One of my favorite shows is Ocurio Asi

which is basically a tabloid but there is always some
feature on the bizarre. The other day they had the
lady with the longest tongue in the world. Another
program featured some guy in Mexico who had been
in chains for forty years. My favorite is No Estamos
Solos, about extraterrestrials. On Sunday is Siempre
en Domingo. They always have all the great singers
new and old, and bandas, etc. It always amazes me
how they can have someone like Lola Beltran
followed by the latest rockeros. Which reminds me
to tell you I have a new friend. Her name is
Wednesday though everybody calls her Wendy. Her
mother gave her that name since she was a big fan
of the actress Tuesday Weld but didn't want her
daughter to have exactly the same name so she
changed it by one day. Wendy is seventeen and a
rockera. I met her at a mall where she works at a
coffee stand. She is a half breed with green eyes like
me. She has bleached blond hair because she wants
to look like Paulina Rubio, but talks like a chola. She
says I look like Audrey Hepburn and that's "bad".
She is going soon to D. F. and I told her all the best
places to buy good shoes, something she is very
excited about. She says she is going down there for
her boyfriend's cousin's wedding and it's gonna be
"so bad". Her boyfriend is a lowrider. He has three

but no Impalas. I asked her why no Impalas and she said Man, those are for cholos. I asked her if her boyfriend was a cholo because in my closed mind lowriders are for cholos and she goes No way, we're rockeros. I meet someone I like about once a year and as far as I can remember she is it for this year. At the mall where I met Wendy a man and a woman from the newspaper were asking people what their biggest wish in life was. A woman said To be happy with my kids and without a husband because he don't work for me. They asked me and Wendy. Wendy said To get my own place and for my boyfriend to not be so flaky. I said To always stay friends with my best girlfriends so we can get together to whore around. If it gets in the newspaper I'll cut it out and send it to you.

My biggest problems here are mosquitos and weather. The weather makes you feel horny all the time but you don't want to do anything about it. Too hot. And the air conditioning is not romantic at all, it makes you lose the concentration. I went to a carnival yesterday. What a pain in the ass and I was dumb enough to wear three-inch platforms. My feet still hurt. I went with a girl I don't know very well named Chocolate. She kept winning games and making fun of me because I couldn't get a prize.

What a brat. I think I won't be friends with Chocolate. Would you?

Well, I better blow out the candles now before I burn the house down. Hope to see you soon.

Con mucho cariño
Concha

I, CAIRO FLY

FEBRUARY 4. I, Cairo Fly, begin this diary at the request of my doctor. She has suggested that every day I attempt to record one thought along with a description of the weather. She says this way we will get to know about more than just the weather. All right then, here goes. This morning when I woke up there was a cloud on the ground. In other words it was very foggy. Now it is later and the sun is squirming through. My favorite word of all is romántico. Spanish for romantic.

FEBRUARY 5. I watched the dawn come up pure. The light was perfect across the horizon like a pencil line made with a ruler, it was so straight and red. I did not murder anybody.

FEBRUARY 6. The sky is full of stratocumulus clouds. These are low altitude white-to-gray water droplet clouds that cover a widespread area probably hundreds of miles. My mother named me Cairo, pronounced Kay-ro, after the town in Illinois where I was born. We lived there until I was three, then we moved to New Orleans.

FEBRUARY 7. Chinook winds gusted up to 123 miles per hour yesterday in Colorado, I heard on the radio. It was Tondelayo Luna shot those folks. I didn't even know she had a gun. I was just along for the ride.

FEBRUARY 8. Snow fell on most of northern Alabama. It was so heavy in some places it crushed chicken houses, killing hundreds of thousands of chickens. Hard for me to believe I am 43 years old. I would say I am much younger when asked. Tondelayo was 22 when she was put on Death Row, where she is rotting. I am told this state has never executed a woman.

FEBRUARY 9. On the television I saw film of an avalanche as it buried several houses on a mountainside in Utah. Why anyone would build a house in a place like that makes me wonder about *their* sanity, not mine. I wonder too if my mama hadn't just left me like she did in N.O. when I was twelve years old, would my life have been so different. Tondelayo used to say not to think about might or maybe. Maybe she's right.

FEBRUARY 10. I don't like the sun anymore. This has nothing to do with my complexion. This morning it was very cold when I was allowed outdoors for an hour to walk around the grounds, but the sun was very strong. Powerful sunlight no longer suits my mood. When the police found me they put a gun in my right hand and made me get fingerprints on the trigger and grip, then they took it away. Later I told the lawyer I'm left-handed. If I had fired a gun, which I did not, I would have held it in my left hand. I wanted to tell the judge too, but the lawyer told me not to say anything otherwise I would go to regular prison. Rock steady, Cairo, the game ain't altogether over.

FEBRUARY 11. Ice on the Mississippi River today at New Orleans. I've never seen ice on the river there. I'm hearing voices now in my sleep. Not dreams, just voices. I woke up this morning when it was still dark out after a voice said my mama was dead. I don't know if this is true. I haven't known where she is for years. There was a face in the blackness on the other side of the room with a kind of yellow ring around it. The mouth was moving, and sounds came out, but I couldn't understand any words. I closed my eyes, and when I opened them again the face had disappeared.

FEBRUARY 12. Big winds caused a ship to capsize off Point Sur on the California coast, which is pretty unusual I guess. I remember how windy it was the day Tondelayo took me with her to watch her get tattooed. She got a grinning skull with lightning bolts coming out of the eyes drawn on her abdomen. That way she said whoever went down on her would see the deathshead and know what she was about and what they were getting into, ha-ha.

FEBRUARY 13. Unusually warm in Maine and the rest of New England. I read the weather page in the newspaper now. I don't look out the window some days because it doesn't seem to matter if I can't go where I want. A man and a woman are dead because of me even though I did not kill them myself maybe I could have stopped her. It happened so fast. Tomorrow is the day.

FEBRUARY 27. I couldn't write for two weeks, being
so low feeling, thinking of the murders. Now there
are a few white blossoms on the cherry trees here.
Yesterday hail fell on the Farasan Islands in the Red
Sea for the first time in history they know about.
Those people who live there must have thought the
sky was breaking apart.

FEBRUARY 28. I recall when I was playing piano in a
club called Chicken in a Basket on Diversey Street in
Chicago, where older gentlemen went to meet
young boys, there was a snowstorm that trapped
everyone inside for almost two days. Wasn't that a
time. If men could get pregnant nine months to that
day later there would have been panic in the
maternity wards of hospitals all over the city.

MARCH 1. I never can remember that bit of business
with the groundhog and its shadow seeing it or not
and how long the winter will be. Anyhow today is
very cold even inside with heat. There are some
colors I can't see, especially up next to certain other
colors. A boy in New Orleans found out how I
didn't know if something like a pair of pants was red
or brown and called me Dog Eyes. Dogs are
supposed to be color-blind, but how do they know?

MARCH 2. Floods in Georgia. On TV I saw a small car get covered up by water in about two shakes. Very scary. Tondy sent me a letter asking me to say I think she's crazy, then they won't kill her. How can she be crazy when I know I'm not crazy either?

MARCH 3. On the radio I heard a weatherman say that on this date in 1869 a red snow fell on France that was called the blood snow. It wasn't blood, he said, but red dust blown all the way from the Sahara desert, where windstorms are called siroccos. *Sirocco* is an especially beautiful word, like *romántico*. Tondelayo told me she once stabbed her baby brother while he was asleep just to see what the blood looked like when it ran out of his skin. She was about seven years old at the time and he was two.

MARCH 4. A hurricane hit Australia today, causing shipwrecks and deaths. Sometimes I get thoughts like dreams, only I'm wide awake, like a dog or other animal is chasing me but there isn't. Last night I had a real dream where somebody whispered very loud in my ear. I woke up and my ear hurt and itched like an insect had flown into it. I put a finger

in and rubbed around and I remembered the
whisperer had said, Come outside!

MARCH 5. Very windy today. Birds are being blown
off their path. When Mama left me to myself in
N.O. I didn't believe it was really forever that she
was gone. The cheap psychology of it as the doctor
would say is that Tondy came along and I
substituted her for myself at that young age and
refused to abandon her as my mother did me. So it's
not just because of Tondy that I'm inside. Blame
Mama or myself, I guess. The world won't stop
spinning on none of our account.

MARCH 6. Tornadoes ripped up most of Arkansas
yesterday. The town of Arkadelphia looked about
totally destroyed on the TV news. Did God have it
in for those folks? He did not. It's only people have
it in for each other. Each other being a part of their
very self is what I believe and will bear witness to.
Cruelty begins and ends at home.

MARCH 7. Unseasonably warm and sunny today but
rain on the way they say, like always, the way life
is. Tondy did not ever tell me she had it in for a

man. The police say she used me then and she's using me now and probably they're right since we all use each other. Could you believe this is not true? Could you blame her or anyone had a bad childhood like that? Me included.

MARCH 8. Dust storms hit the Oklahoma and Texas Panhandle, I saw on the news. They said like it did back in the days made everybody get up and move toward California. Mama kept telling me, about every day I knew her, not to trust white people no matter who or how nice they seem. Her experience in life was different from mine. Mostly it's been pretty much a mix between white and black and others has helped or hurt me, and what do we call Tondelyao Luna who is part Samoa and some other island? People you have to take the way they play.

MARCH 9. Kansas is covered in snow. Here there are birds all of a sudden everywhere. Birds are creatures I have always held real interest for. Maybe it's still possible I could study them somewhere. Harry, a Greek guy I had a crush on in Chicago, had a hawk tattoo on his right arm would fly when he made a muscle.

MARCH 10. Mostly tornadoes are in the news, being this particular time of year and floods. Personally I could not live by a river ever anymore. I ever get out of this place I want to be on a mountain top or in a skyscraper. I have an idea to make a movie about my life, but it would have to have a happy ending.

MARCH 11. The lowest temperature ever recorded in the United States as of yesterday's date was 50 degrees below zero at Snake River, Wyoming, in 1906. I would die in that cold of a temperature. When I get out I want to go first to a hot island with nice breezes. I am close to decided about saying I think Tondy is insane.

MARCH 12. Raining, like it said. Tondy would bring guys to fuck and I would rob them while they were with her. They caught me a few times or figured out the deal, but we always got away. Tondy pulled a knife on more than a couple, but I only saw her cut one man. The man was entirely naked except for shoes and she stabbed him in the left leg, going for his dick and balls. He was carrying a lot and we got it.

MARCH 13. Wind gusts of over 50 miles per hour. The men I liked never really paid attention to me, not for my real self. This has made a big difference in what could have been for me in my life. I would like, I think, to be an angel, and maybe that will happen someday even with all my bad behavior.

MARCH 15. First time I had sex was with a stranger in the restroom of a Greyhound bus on the highway north of Memphis. I was 14 drunk and on Quaaludes going from N.O. to Chicago. He was about 40, pulled down my pants, leaned me over the sink, I still remember the cold metal on my stomach. I watched my face in the mirror, the color go brown to red. Tonight the moon is full of blood.

MARCH 19. Sunny all over the country today, but in Japan there was an earthquake. I hope nobody was killed. People are caught up in their own life, no reason they should care what I do unless it affects them.

MARCH 20. I think people act the way they do sometimes because of the weather on a particular day. It was very foggy the night Tondelayo and I got in trouble, kind of like it is this morning but it was worse that night. We saw the couple come out of the store carrying packages, and Tondy said they must be rich and pulled out the gun and went right after them. I didn't even have time to say anything until it was over.

MARCH 25. The sun makes my mind depress. I can't go anywhere under it, so what good is it to me? The world is sometimes so silent I can't hear a thing. I was sick the past few days so I didn't write. I got out of bed to watch a lunar eclipse where it looked like a big black fish swam up from under and swallowed the moon, which I imagne would be a thrilling feeling, being swallowed up alive.

MARCH 26. Hailstorms in Florida. One knocked out a 17-year-old boy who was crazy enough to be out in it. I signed the paper with my opinion that Tondy is insane. If they think I'm insane, what does it matter but it could help save her life. I don't believe they would kill a woman anyway.

APRIL 1. Nothing but rain now for several days. I have not written because of feeling low. Is it possible for a person's soul to stray away or be stolen and without it the person has no peace in their heart? I feel I am one of those now.

Dear Cairo

I am down in a bad place without no sun almost
never. All the girls hear say they wont kill a woman.
Texas and Florida maybe but not hear. You got to be
careful where you do your kapitol crime. Remember
Raoul Colby the older man wanted to marry me?
Well I wrote to him and he promise to pay for a
lawyer who could get me out if I would marry him.
I said yes I would who wouldnt? My first boyfrend
Ralph Deacon would drive around with a gun under
a towel on the floor of his car so he could just reach
down and grab it when he needed. I liked Ralph he
was a real freek when it come to sex. He liked for
me to pee on his chest after we done it. I bet Ralph
is dead today. You and me wont be though now they
know we crazy. My only question is if we ever goin
to get out? The girls in here say it aint likely. Maybe
when we just pieces of dried up fruit cant harm
nobody. What harm we do Cairo any way? Nobody
kill was no good you know it I know it they know
it. We meet up face to face baby I hold you tight.

Love

Tondy

The Wild Life of Sailor and Lula
Barry Gifford

Featuring the novels *WILD AT HEART, PERDITA DURANGO,
SAILOR'S HOLIDAY, SULTANS OF AFRICA, CONSUELO'S
KISS and BAD DAY FOR THE LEOPARD MAN*

**Published together for the first time in the
English language, *The Wild Life of Sailor and
Lula* presents Barry Gifford's meisterwork as
originally intended - six interlocking novels
charting the wild lives of Sailor Ripley and
Lula Pace Fortune, the most likeable, sex-
driven, star-crossed lovers that you are ever
going to meet.**

**"A dark and comic ride through a fantasy
America that rings desperately true."**
                    The New York Times Book Review

**"Gifford cuts right to the heart of what
makes a good novel readable and
entertaining : the voices of real people. The
way he does it, it's high art."**
                                    Elmore Leonard

**"If you bemoan the lack of something
'different' in fiction, your search is over."**
                                    Andrew Vachs